ENOLA

Enola

Evelyn Wong

Published by Evelyn Wong, 2025.

This is a work of fiction. Similarities to real people, places, or events are entirely coincidental.

ENOLA

First edition. January 14, 2025.

Copyright © 2025 Evelyn Wong.

ISBN: 979-8227528292

Written by Evelyn Wong.

Table of Contents

Chapter 1 1
Chapter 2 7
Chapter 3 11
Chapter 4 15
Chapter 5 19
Chapter 6 23
Chapter 7 28
Chapter 8 33
Chapter 9 37
Chapter 10 42
Chapter 11 46
Chapter 12 51
Chapter 13 54
Chapter 14 58
Chapter 15 62
Chapter 16 66
Chapter 17 71
Chapter 18 76
Chapter 19 80
Chapter 20 84
Chapter 21 88
Chapter 22 92
Chapter 23 96
Chapter 24 101
Chapter 25 106
Chapter 26 109
Chapter 27 114
Chapter 28 119
Chapter 29 124

Chapter 30 128

To my family, who supplied me with endless ideas,
unwavering love and support that made this possible.

Chapter 1

One by one, the lights in the town centre flickered and died. A lone taxi carried away its last ride, leaving the city to sink into sleep. The streets, once bustling with the hum of activity, now lay still. An eerie silence enveloped the city, broken only by the occasional distant sound of a car engine. Shadows crept out from the darkened alleys, wrapping themselves around the worn buildings, as the night deepened.

Suddenly, a door crashed open, the sharp sound cutting through the stillness. A pool of harsh yellow light spilled out, revealing a line of dirty bins huddled outside. The pungent smell of rotting food wafted into the night, but it barely fazed Enola. She had long learned to tolerate such odours—her life in the streets had taught her how to survive in the grime and filth that most people would never dare to touch.

Enola flinched and sank deeper into the shadows of Little Vixon Street, her amber eyes narrowing as she watched the figure step into the light. She was quick to melt into the darkness, her body blending seamlessly with the surroundings. Her fur, a pitch-dark with patches of brown. / and gold, seemed to merge with the shadows, leaving her almost invisible.

The figure emerged from the doorway, the stench of the night thick around them. In one swift motion, they tossed a rancid carcass into the bin and slammed the door shut behind them. The sound reverberated through the alley, and the street was plunged into darkness once more, the harsh light vanishing as quickly as it had appeared.

Enola's ears flicked. She could hear the soft rustle of wind in the trees and the faint whisper of traffic in the distance, but most of all, she could hear her stomach growling. Hunger gnawed at her, a constant companion that never seemed to leave. It had been days since her last real meal, and the sight of that carcass, discarded without a second thought, was enough to make her pulse quicken.

She hesitated, her eyes scanning the alley for any signs of movement. The street was deserted, but there was always the chance that someone—or something—might appear at any moment. Still, the hunger was too much to ignore. With a soft, silent tread, she moved toward the overturned bin, her nose twitching as the delicious scent of chicken wafted into her nostrils. The smell was irresistible, and for a moment, she forgot everything else—the shadows, the danger, the city. All that mattered was the food, and the warmth of the meat that still clung to the bones.

Her claws scraped against the metal of the bin as she dug deeper, her eyes wide in anticipation. She could feel the meat beneath her paws—tender, juicy, perfect. But then, as her claws brushed the soft flesh, a noise interrupted her.

A can clattered, rolled and stopped near her paws. Enola froze, her heart leaping in her chest. She quickly flattened herself against the wall, her amber eyes wide as she scanned the darkness. The hairs on her back stood on end. She had been so focused on the food that she hadn't noticed the figure lingering in the shadows nearby.

The light above her flickered once—twice—and then died. But just as quickly, it flickered back to life, casting a long, jagged shadow on the ground. The shadow stretched out before her, elongating as the flickering bulb above her cast an eerie light. It looked like skeletal fingers reaching toward her, scraping and clawing at the pavement with an unnatural, slow deliberation.

Enola's breath caught in her throat as she saw the creature for the first time. Its eyes glowed with an eerie, porcelain light, reflecting the dim glow of the streetlamp above. The creature's claws scraped across the concrete, dragging in a slow, deliberate motion that sent a shiver down Enola's spine. The growl it emitted was inhuman, a deep, rumbling sound that seemed to vibrate the very air around her. It was a sound that wasn't meant for this world—a sound that shouldn't exist.

Panic surged through her veins. Her heart pounded in her chest as she scrambled away from the bin, her body acting on instinct. She ran as fast as her legs could carry her, darting into the shadows of the alley. She could hear the creature's footsteps behind her, growing louder, faster. The air was thick with its presence, a palpable sense of danger that sent a chill down her spine.

The creature's growls grew louder, its breathing ragged and heavy. Enola could hear the desperation in its movements, the urgency of its pursuit. The hairs along her back stood on end as she pushed herself harder, her legs aching with the strain. The street stretched out before her, a maze of dark alleyways and crumbling buildings, but she knew she had to keep moving. She couldn't stop—not now.

Then—**bang!**

A deafening noise split the silence of the night, so loud it felt as though the very air had been torn apart. Enola flinched, her teeth rattling from the shockwave. The sound was like a knife carving into rotten flesh, a noise so horrible that it rattled her bones. For a moment, everything went still, and the world seemed to stop moving.

In that moment of stunned silence, Enola didn't hesitate. She bolted, her body streaking through the dark alley as she searched for safety. Her heart raced in her chest, her breath coming in sharp, panicked gasps. She slammed into the side of a rusted chain-link fence, her paws digging into the dirt as she pressed her body against it. She turned, her wide eyes searching the shadows, waiting for the creature to emerge.

It didn't.

The creature had disappeared into the darkness, its growls fading into the distance. But Enola didn't dare relax. She couldn't afford to. Her heart still thudded in her chest, and her stomach twisted with anxiety. She couldn't go back to the carcass—not now. The creature had scared it away, but there was something more at play here. Something she didn't understand.

Enola stayed pressed against the fence, watching the shadows for any sign of movement. Her breath came in shallow, rapid bursts, the fear still clinging to her like a second skin. The creature was gone, but she could still feel it in the air, lurking just beyond the edge of her awareness.

After what felt like an eternity, Enola forced herself to breathe, calming the rapid pace of her heart. She glanced over her shoulder once more to make sure she was still alone. With one last look, she pushed herself away from the fence and padded silently back into the alley.

The streets were still silent, the only sounds the distant hum of the city and the faint rustle of wind through the trees. The flickering streetlights cast long, ghostly shadows that seemed to stretch forever into the darkness. Enola licked her lips, tasting the remnants of the chicken on her tongue. Her stomach growled in protest, but she knew better than to try again. Not tonight.

With a cautious glance to ensure she was still alone, Enola moved deeper into Little Vixon Street. The alleyways here were a maze—twisted passageways, abandoned shops, and crumbling brick walls that had stood for years, weathered by time. It was here, among the ruins, that Enola felt most at home.

She could sense it again—the movement ahead. A figure. A silhouette crouched low, half-hidden in the shadow of a doorway. Enola froze, her muscles tensing. Her amber eyes narrowed as she focused on the figure, her mind racing. It wasn't the creature—not this time. But who was it?

She stepped forward cautiously, one paw after the other, her breath shallow as she tried to stay as quiet as possible. The smell of decay filled the air, thick and rancid, but there was something else now—something metallic, like the scent of blood. Enola stopped just before the corner, her body hidden behind a rusted dumpster. The figure hadn't moved, but something felt off about it.

The air around the figure felt... wrong. Enola couldn't explain it, but there was a sense of unease, a feeling that something wasn't quite right. Then, before she could make a move, the figure vanished into the darkness.

One moment, it was there—a shadow in the dark—and the next, it was gone. No movement. No sound. Nothing. Enola blinked, her mind racing. She stepped into the open, scanning every corner, every crevice for any sign of life. But there was nothing.

Her heart raced again, her instincts screaming at her to run, to get out of there. But her paws were rooted to the ground. She couldn't shake the feeling that something wasn't right—that she wasn't alone.

A sudden rustling—a whisper of movement—made her jump. Her eyes shot toward the sound, her fur bristling. She felt it now, the eyes on her, watching her from the shadows. She wasn't alone.

Chapter 2

A pale dawn broke over the city, washing its worn streets in cold light. Rain had softened to a drizzle, and the city seemed to stretch its limbs in the wake of the night. But even in the quiet hours of the morning, Little Vixon Street remained untouched by the glow of daylight.

Enola's fur was damp, her body sore from the night spent hidden beneath a discarded mattress. Hunger gnawed at her belly, and the memory of the warm chicken carcass was a cruel tease. Her ears twitched at every creak and groan of the city waking up, but the weight of exhaustion pressed her into the damp ground.

She stretched her legs, her muscles tight and reluctant, and crept out from her makeshift shelter. The rain had cleansed the streets, but it also carried the night's scents away, leaving the air cold and sterile. The familiar smell of rot, oil, and decay had returned with the damp bricks, grounding her in the strange comfort of her territory.

She padded carefully toward the edges of the alley, her nose low to the ground as she searched for any sign of food. The bins had already been emptied, their metallic clangs echoing earlier in the dawn, and the few scraps left behind were sodden and sour. Her stomach growled in protest as she scraped at a corner, uncovering nothing but wet, limp paper.

A faint sound prickled her ears—a rhythmic tapping, distant and almost masked by the rain's patter. Enola froze, her fur standing on end. It wasn't the sound of wind, nor the hollow drip of water. It was deliberate. Too deliberate.

The tapping stopped. Enola's amber eyes darted to the end of the alley, where the shadows lingered longer, as if reluctant to let go of the night. Nothing moved, but the air felt different—heavier, sharper. She took a cautious step forward, her claws unsheathing instinctively against the damp concrete.

The sound returned, this time closer: a sharp clink, like nails dragging across metal. It echoed once, then was swallowed by the damp silence.

Enola's heart began to race. She backed up, her movements slow and measured, until her tail brushed against the edge of the dumpster she'd slept behind. The tapping resumed, uneven and erratic, accompanied by a faint hum—low and guttural, vibrating the air.

It was no longer distant.

Her muscles coiled, ready to run, as the tapping grew louder, sharper. Then it stopped, leaving a void so deafeningly quiet that even the rain seemed to hold its breath.

She turned, her eyes scanning the alley frantically. And there, just beyond the edge of the light, it appeared. A faint glimmer—soft and pale—hovering in the gloom. It was unlike any light she had seen before, pulsing faintly like a heartbeat, growing stronger with each pulse.

Enola froze, her breath shallow, as the light began to move. It wasn't steady—it swayed, shifting left and right, as if searching for something.

For her.

Her claws scraped against the ground as the light grew closer, illuminating the slick pavement in jagged flashes. Enola's legs trembled, but she didn't dare move. The light was alive, deliberate, and inching closer with every breath she took.

And then, from the darkness behind her, came the sound she dreaded most—a low growl, deep and resonant, vibrating through her very bones.

Her pulse surged, her instincts screamed, but before she could react, the growl grew louder, surrounding her, and the light flared, casting her shadow long and sharp against the alley walls.

Enola bolted.

The air around her felt electric, thick with danger as she tore down the alleyway. Her paws splashed through shallow puddles, her heart pounding in her chest. She didn't look back—couldn't. The growl and the pulsing light were chasing her, closing the distance with terrifying speed.

Just ahead, the alley split into two paths. Enola veered left without thinking, her claws scraping against the slippery concrete. The growl followed, closer now, echoing through the narrow walls like a predator closing in on its prey.

The glimmer of light rounded the corner, brighter and sharper now, slicing through the shadows with an unnatural intensity. Enola's legs burned with the effort, but she kept running, weaving through the maze-like streets with the desperation of an animal that knew it was being hunted.

She turned another corner, her paws slipping beneath her. The world spun as she tumbled forward, slamming against the damp ground. Pain flared in her shoulder, but she scrambled to her feet, her breath ragged and uneven. The light was there, seeping into the alley like a tide.

She stumbled backward, her eyes wide as the glow filled the narrow passage, blinding her. A shape began to form within the light, indistinct but menacing, its movements slow and deliberate. It stepped forward, and for the briefest moment, Enola saw it clearly: jagged limbs, a mouth that seemed to twist in ways it shouldn't, and eyes—cold, porcelain eyes that stared through her.

The growl became a roar.

Enola turned and ran, but the alley ended in a dead stop—a brick wall towering above her. She spun around, her back pressed against the cold surface as the light bore down on her. There was nowhere left to run.

The roar echoed once more, shaking the very ground beneath her paws. And then—

Darkness.

Chapter 3

The cold air bit at Enola's skin as she blinked against the blurry light filtering through the cracks in the alley. Her head throbbed, each pulse sharp with the remnants of the terror that had swallowed her whole. She couldn't remember how long she had been unconscious, but the rough stone beneath her body and the dampness seeping into her fur made it clear: she was no longer in the alley where she'd last been.

Enola's eyes fluttered open, her amber gaze catching the faint glow of a flickering streetlamp. She was in a new place—an old warehouse, the wooden beams of the ceiling warped with age. The stench of decay mixed with something sharper, like the tang of blood that lingered in the air. But there was something else: the warmth of living, breathing bodies. Soft murmurs echoed through the shadows.

As she tried to push herself up, her body ached, and she winced at the sharp pain in her side. It was then she noticed the scent of other cats, too many to count. The air hummed with the soft vibrations of a quiet conversation—one she was not part of.

A soft paw nudged her shoulder.

"Easy there, stranger," a voice rumbled—a low, gentle voice, but with the unmistakable edge of authority. Enola turned her head and saw a large tabby cat sitting at her side, eyes glinting in the dark. "You took quite the fall. Good thing we found you when we did."

Enola's throat tightened, her pulse spiking at the realization that she wasn't alone.

"You're safe," the tabby added, his voice reassuring but firm. "We don't get many like you around here, not since... well, since the last incident. But you're in our territory now."

Enola's mouth dried. Territory. The word sent a ripple of unease through her. She had heard the rumours—stray cats banding together, territories divided, the danger of being alone. But there was something in the tabby's gaze that made her want to trust him. There was kindness there, even if it was hard to understand.

"Who... are you?" Enola croaked, her voice hoarse. She licked her lips, trying to gather the strength to sit up properly.

"I'm Korr," the tabby said, flicking his tail, his gaze never leaving hers. "And this is our haven. We're the Strays—don't let the name fool you, we're a family here. You've been unconscious for a while. We had to move you from the alley before the worst found you." He glanced over his shoulder at a dark corner where more cats sat, their eyes gleaming like silent sentinels.

Enola's mind was still foggy, but something in Korr's tone told her she wasn't just being taken care of out of kindness. These cats had a reason, a purpose. And maybe—just maybe—she had stumbled into something bigger than herself.

One of the other cats, a sleek black feline with a jagged scar across his face, padded closer, his eyes narrowing as they met Enola's. "She's awake," he said in a low growl, his voice rough. "Korr, we shouldn't be taking in every stray that stumbles in. What if—"

Korr raised a paw, cutting him off. "Enough, Caden. She's one of us now. I can sense it."

Enola's stomach churned, the remnants of the creature's pursuit still gnawing at her. The memories flashed in her mind like fragmented images—those cold, porcelain eyes, the growl that had sent her into a panic. It wasn't just the physical exhaustion that left her shaking. Something far darker was lingering in the shadows, and it felt like it was getting closer.

"But..." Enola started, her voice trembling, "There was something—something chasing me. I don't know what it was. It wasn't... it wasn't like anything I've ever seen."

At that, the cats fell silent. Even the flickering light seemed to grow dimmer, as though holding its breath. Caden's eyes hardened.

"You're not the first to see it," Korr said softly. "We've all felt it, too. It's been getting worse, and you're right to be afraid. Whatever it is, it's drawn to us—the strays, the lost ones." He paused, glancing toward the dark corners of the room where the other cats were waiting. "We've been keeping it at bay, but the question is... how much longer can we hold it off?"

Enola felt her chest tighten as her mind raced to piece the fragments of her fear together. The creature, the growl, the light—everything had felt wrong, like a threat that was waiting for her, watching, hunting.

"You're not alone in this, Enola," Korr said, his voice suddenly sharp, as though sensing her growing panic. "We'll keep you safe, but we need to work together. This threat—it's real. And it's coming for all of us."

The air seemed to grow colder, the shadows deeper. Enola's breath quickened, the realization dawning on her with sudden clarity. The Strays might have helped her, but the danger wasn't over. In fact, it was just beginning.

She opened her mouth to speak, but before she could, the door to the warehouse creaked open with an eerie groan.

Every cat in the room froze. Korr's eyes widened, a flicker of panic passing through them. He bolted to his paws.

Something was outside. Something was here.

Enola's heart skipped a beat, her body tense, every nerve alive with the thrum of impending danger.

A soft meow echoed from the doorway, and then a voice she didn't recognize cut through the silence:

"I'm sorry... but you need to hear this."

Chapter 4

The door creaked open, and the room held its breath. Enola's fur stood on end as the soft, pleading meow echoed through the air. Her eyes darted to Korr, who stood frozen, a low growl rumbling deep in his throat. The other cats had begun to shift restlessly, their ears flicking nervously, tails twitching with unease.

Enola's heartbeat thundered in her chest. Whoever—or whatever—was on the other side of that door, she knew they were not here for a friendly visit.

"I'm sorry," the voice said again, the tone strained, as though it had fought its way through something painful. It was faint but carried an unmistakable sense of urgency. "But you need to hear this."

The air was thick with tension as the door slowly opened wider, revealing the figure of a small, scruffy cat standing in the frame. Her fur was matted, a mix of brown and grey, and her eyes gleamed with a strange, unsettling intensity. She was panting as if she had run for miles, her breath coming in sharp bursts.

Enola felt the hairs on the back of her neck prickle. There was something off about the newcomer, something that stirred her instincts.

The tabby, Korr, took a step forward, his tail bristling. "Who are you?" he demanded. "What do you want?"

The cat at the door lowered her head in respect, but there was a tremor in her voice when she spoke. "My name is Veda," she said, her voice cracking slightly. "I've come to warn you."

Enola's eyes narrowed, her mind racing with questions. A warning? She had no idea who this cat was or what she meant, but the sense of urgency in her tone sent a shiver down Enola's spine.

Veda stepped into the room, her movements quick and jittery, her eyes flicking over the faces of the other cats. She paused, as if trying to gauge who to trust before she continued.

"The creature," Veda said in a low, trembling voice. "It's not just hunting the strays... It's after something more. Something much worse. You all need to understand what's coming."

Enola felt the air grow colder, her pulse quickening. The creature she had faced in the alley—the one with the glowing eyes—wasn't just some random threat. It had a purpose. And now this strange cat, Veda, was claiming there was more to the danger.

"What do you mean?" Korr growled, his tone sharp. "What is it after?"

Veda's eyes shifted nervously toward the dark corners of the warehouse, and she took a step closer to Korr. "It's after... the last of us. The last of the 'wild.' You see, this creature—it's not just hunting strays for food or sport. It's hunting the soul of what we are—the last of the free cats. It feeds on us. It's an ancient thing, older than most of the stories we hear."

Enola's chest tightened at the words, her mind struggling to grasp their full meaning. The creature didn't just want them—it was after something much deeper. But why?

"The Strays," Veda continued, glancing nervously at Enola, "are the last line of defence. It will come for us first. We can't outrun it. We can't hide from it. And the more it takes, the stronger it grows. The closer it gets to wiping out all of us—the true free cats. And once it's done with us... it will move on to others. The world itself. It's only a matter of time."

Enola felt a knot of dread tighten in her stomach. She had always known the streets were dangerous, that life as a stray was full of threats, but this... this was different. This wasn't about food, or territory, or even survival. This was something ancient, something beyond her comprehension.

Her voice was barely a whisper. "So. what can we do?"

Veda looked at her, her eyes filled with sorrow and urgency. "We fight," she said, her voice steady now, as though she had made up her mind. "We gather the others. We make our stand. But we can't do it alone. We need to know what it is, where it comes from, and how to stop it before it takes everything."

The room fell silent. Every cat's eyes were on Veda, their bodies tense, as if waiting for the next move.

Enola swallowed hard, her mind racing. She had no idea how they would fight something like this, something so powerful and terrifying. But one thing was clear: it wasn't just about survival anymore. This was about something much larger than any of them.

Korr spoke up, his voice firm but with an edge of disbelief. "How do we fight something like that? You say it's ancient. You say it feeds on us. But how do we stop it? Tell us that, Veda."

Veda looked back at the door, her eyes shadowed with fear. "I don't know. Not yet. But I do know that if we don't act, it'll come for us all. And when it does, we will not survive."

Enola's heart pounded in her chest as the weight of her words sank in. She had survived one encounter, barely, but there was no telling what would happen next. If the creature was as powerful as Veda claimed, and it truly fed on them like some kind of predator, then they had to prepare.

Veda turned to the door once more, her voice barely audible. "The clock is ticking. We have to move before it finds us again."

And just as the words left her mouth, the door slammed shut behind her with an ominous thud. Every cat in the room jumped, their muscles coiling, their eyes scanning the dark corners once more.

Something else was out there. Something that wasn't just watching. It was waiting.

Chapter 5

The silence that followed Veda's departure was heavy, oppressive. The air in the room felt thick with unease, as if the walls themselves were holding their breath. Enola stood frozen, her eyes fixed on the spot where Veda had vanished. The other cats were just as still, their bodies tense, their ears flicking at every sound, as if expecting the worst to arrive at any moment.

Korr was the first to speak, his voice low and rough, almost a growl. "Do you think she's telling the truth?"

Enola blinked, tearing her gaze away from the door. She had no idea. Veda's words had been a jumbled mess of fear and urgency, but something in her tone, in the way she spoke of the creature, had struck a chord with Enola. It had been too real. Too personal.

"I don't know," she admitted, her voice quiet. "But I think she believes it. And if she's right... then we don't have much time."

A shiver ran through her, and she wrapped her tail around her paws, curling her body tightly. She had always known the city was full of dangers—rats, other territorial cats, the occasional dog—but this was something different. Something far worse than anything she could have ever imagined.

Korr paced back and forth, his paws tapping against the cold concrete floor. "We need a plan," he muttered, his eyes flicking toward the others. "If we're going to fight this thing, we can't just sit around waiting to be picked off one by one."

Enola nodded slowly. She didn't know where to begin, but she knew they couldn't face this alone. They had to find others—other strays who had survived in the city for years, who knew the streets, who could help them. But where? Who could they trust?

Her thoughts were interrupted by a low, familiar voice from the corner of the room.

"We'll need more than just numbers."

Enola turned toward the voice, her eyes narrowing as she saw a lanky grey tom sitting with his back to the wall, his green eyes glowing in the dim light. Rook. Enola had met him a few times before—an odd cat with a sharp tongue and a tendency to be alone. He was clever, but there was always a sense of distance about him, as if he didn't fully belong with the others.

Rook's eyes flicked to each cat in turn, his gaze lingering on Enola for a moment before he spoke again. "It's not just about gathering a group. It's about finding the right kind of help."

Korr snorted, his lip curling. "What are you saying? We need all the help we can get."

Rook tilted his head, his expression unreadable. "That's where you're wrong. Not all help is good help. Some cats are dangerous. Some are worse than the creatures hunting us."

Enola's fur bristled at the mention of "worse," but she kept quiet. This wasn't the time to argue with Rook. He was right, in a way—there were always those cats who lived by their own rules, who didn't care about the community of strays. The kind who would sell you out for a scrap of food or turn on you if it meant their own survival.

"I agree," Enola said softly, her voice steady despite the uncertainty crawling up her spine. "But we can't do it alone. We need to trust someone."

Rook stared at her for a long moment before slowly nodding. "Fine. But you'd better make sure they're worth it."

Enola let out a slow breath. "I know."

There was a heavy pause as the weight of their words settled over the group. They couldn't waste time arguing. If the creature was as dangerous as Veda said, they needed to act quickly. And the first step was finding the others—cats who could fight, who knew the city and its dangers. Enola wasn't sure where to start, but she knew one thing for certain: the hunt was already on.

"We'll start in the east," Korr said suddenly, his voice cutting through the silence. "That's where the oldest of the strays tend to hide—those who have been around long enough to know the city's secrets. If anyone can help us, it'll be them."

Enola nodded. She had heard of the elder strays before. The ones who lived in the abandoned factories and underground tunnels, far from the prying eyes of the city. They were mysterious, elusive, and no one really knew much about them. Some said they were survivors of an old war, others claimed they were witches, using magic to keep themselves safe. Whatever the truth was, they were their best bet.

"I'll go," Enola said, her voice firm. "We'll need to find them before the creature does. Korr, you stay here and keep watch. Rook, you're coming with me."

Rook raised an eyebrow. "You want me to go with you?"

Enola met his gaze, her amber eyes steady. "You're the only one who knows the city well enough. If we're going to find the elders, you're our best chance."

Rook didn't answer immediately. Instead, he stood up slowly, stretching his long legs. "Fine," he muttered. "But don't expect me to be friendly about it."

Enola gave a slight nod, her pulse quickening as the weight of their decision settled over her. They were on their own now, and the path ahead was uncertain, dangerous. But one thing was clear: there was no turning back. The creature was coming, and they had to be ready.

As they left the room, stepping into the narrow streets of the city, Enola's mind raced. The day was just beginning to break, the first light of dawn casting long shadows across the buildings. The world felt cold and silent, like it was holding its breath.

And then, a sound—a faint rustling from the alleyway ahead. Enola stopped, her body going rigid, her eyes narrowing in suspicion. Rook tensed beside her, his tail flicking nervously. Something was there. Something watching them.

Enola took a deep breath, her senses sharpening. She was no stranger to danger, but this... this felt different. There was no creature chasing them this time. No growling in the shadows.

Just the unsettling silence.

The rustling grew louder, closer. Something—or someone—was out there, waiting.

Chapter 6

The rustling sound grew louder, too distinct to be ignored. It was coming from the dark alleyway just ahead, the one where the crumbling buildings and twisted metal scraps seemed to whisper with age. Enola's heart raced as she instinctively shifted her weight to the balls of her paws, ready to spring into action if necessary.

Rook's eyes narrowed as he listened. "It's not just the wind," he muttered, his voice low and tense. "Something's out there."

Enola's fur stood on end. "Stay close," she whispered, more to herself than to Rook, though she could feel the tom's presence behind her, his muscles coiled in silent readiness.

The sound stopped abruptly. Silence.

Enola's breath caught in her throat. The stillness was almost worse than the noise. She could feel her heart pounding in her chest, each beat thunderous in her ears. She wanted to move forward, to investigate, but every instinct told her to wait. To be patient.

Rook, however, wasn't waiting. He took a step forward, then another, his claws scraping quietly against the pavement. Enola followed him cautiously, every sense alert, every muscle tight.

Then, from the shadows ahead, a voice broke the silence.

"Thought you might be coming."

Enola froze. The voice was deep, rough, and unlike any she had ever heard before. There was no mistaking the command in it, the sense of authority. But it wasn't a threat. It was more like an invitation—one she couldn't refuse even if she wanted to.

"Who's there?" Enola demanded, her voice steady but wary. She wasn't sure what to expect, but she knew better than to approach a stranger without caution.

From the shadows, a large, dark figure emerged slowly, stepping into the dim light of the street. Enola's first instinct was to retreat, but she stood her ground, her amber eyes narrowing as the figure came closer.

It was a cat, but not one she recognized. The tom was enormous, his fur black as night, with a thick coat that made him look even larger. His eyes gleamed a piercing yellow, almost glowing in the fading light of dawn. There was something unnerving about him, something primal in the way he carried himself.

"Relax," the tom said with a small, wry smile. "I'm not here to hurt you."

"Who are you?" Enola asked, her voice sharper now. She wasn't about to let her guard down so easily, especially not with someone so strange—and so imposing—in front of her.

The tom cocked his head slightly, his gaze lingering on her for a moment before he spoke again. "Names don't matter much around here. Not when you're dealing with the kind of trouble that's lurking in the shadows. I've been watching you."

Enola's eyes widened. "Watching me?"

"Not just you," he replied. "Watching all of you. All the strays in the city. I know what's coming."

Enola's fur prickled. "How do you know about that?"

The tom's expression darkened, his yellow eyes flickering with something Enola couldn't place. "Let's just say... I've been around long enough to know when things are about to go wrong. And trust me, it's coming. It's already here."

Rook stepped forward, his ears flat, eyes narrowed. "What are you talking about?"

"The creature," the tom said simply, his voice a low growl. "The one that's hunting you."

Enola's heart skipped a beat. How could he know about that? No one, not even Veda, had told anyone else. The word was still too fresh in her mind, and yet this stranger was speaking of it like it was already a known fact. A threat everyone was aware of.

"How do you know about it?" she asked, her voice trembling despite her best efforts to keep it steady.

The tom didn't answer right away. He simply stared at her, a long, considering look. Then, without a word, he turned and motioned for them to follow him.

"Come," he said, his tone both commanding and calm. "You need to see something."

Enola hesitated for a moment. She didn't trust this cat, didn't trust his cryptic words, but she didn't have much of a choice. The creature was coming for them, and if this tom really knew something they didn't, they had to listen.

Rook shot her a glance, his eyes full of scepticism, but after a beat, he nodded. "Lead the way."

They followed him down the narrow street, turning a corner and slipping into a dark alley that led deeper into the heart of the city. The buildings here were taller, their windows long since shattered, their metal frames rusted and decaying. The air smelled of mildew and old refuse, and the sound of distant traffic was drowned out by the muffled hum of the city's underbelly.

After a few minutes, the tom stopped in front of a broken-down building, its door hanging crookedly from one hinge. He motioned for them to enter, and Enola felt a chill settle in her bones. There was something about this place—the way it loomed in the shadows, how everything seemed to be watching them—that felt wrong.

As they stepped inside, the first thing Enola noticed was the smell. It wasn't the usual scent of dampness and decay. No, this was different. It was sharp, metallic—like blood.

The tom moved forward without hesitation, and Enola followed, her eyes scanning the room. The walls were covered in strange markings, symbols she didn't recognize, and the floor was littered with old papers and broken glass. But it wasn't the mess that caught her attention.

It was the centre of the room. There, in the middle, was a large, circular symbol, etched into the ground. The air around it felt charged, heavy, as if something dark and ancient had been disturbed.

"Step closer," the tom said, his voice soft but insistent. "And see for yourselves."

Enola hesitated but then stepped forward, her paws sinking into the cold, cracked floor. She felt a sudden shiver run down her spine as the room seemed to close in around her. The shadows seemed to grow deeper, darker, and the symbol at the centre of the room seemed to pulse with a strange energy.

"What is this?" Enola whispered, her voice trembling with a mix of fear and curiosity.

The tom's yellow eyes gleamed as he turned to her. "This is where it begins."

Suddenly, a low, guttural growl filled the room. It wasn't the sound of the creature—but something else, something far worse.

Enola's breath caught in her throat. The creature wasn't the only danger they faced. Something else was stirring in the darkness, something far older—and much more deadly.

Chapter 7

The air in the room seemed to thicken with each passing second, the growl reverberating in the corners like a low rumble of thunder. Enola's fur stood on end as she searched the shadows, her heart hammering in her chest. The tom remained still, his piercing yellow eyes locked onto the centre of the symbol as if waiting for something to emerge.

Rook's fur bristled beside her. "What is that sound?" he asked, his voice tense. "It's not the creature, is it?"

The tom didn't answer immediately, his gaze unwavering. The growl grew louder, closer now, echoing through the room like the growl of a beast trapped in the depths of the earth. Enola took a step back, her ears pinned flat against her skull, the tension in the air making her skin crawl.

Then, without warning, the symbol on the floor began to glow. It wasn't a flash of light—it was a steady, unnatural glow, flickering like a candle flame struggling to stay lit. Enola's pulse quickened. Something was happening. Something dangerous.

"What's happening?" Enola demanded, her voice rising slightly. "What's coming?"

The tom turned to face her, his expression as unreadable as ever. "Something much older than the creature you've seen. Something much worse."

Before Enola could ask him what he meant, the growl erupted into a deafening roar. The room seemed to shake as the air itself warped, the very walls trembling under the force of it. The glowing symbol flared brighter, casting eerie shadows on the walls. Enola felt a deep, primal fear rise in her chest. It was no longer just the creature she had to fear—it was whatever this thing was.

Rook took a step forward, his eyes narrowed, but Enola stopped him with a sharp look. She had no idea what they were facing, but it was clear that this was something neither of them were prepared for.

"Stay back," the tom said, his voice low but firm. "This is not a battle for you to fight. Not yet."

Enola's fur prickled. "What do you mean, not yet? What is this thing?"

The tom didn't respond. Instead, he stepped closer to the symbol on the floor, his eyes fixed on it with an intensity that made Enola feel small and insignificant. His tail flicked behind him, and for a moment, Enola thought she saw something move in the shadows. Something large, something ancient.

Then, with a sudden burst of energy, the ground beneath them cracked open, sending shards of stone flying into the air. Enola jumped back, her heart racing as the room seemed to collapse inward. The symbol in the centre of the floor was now fully alive, glowing with an almost blinding intensity, and from the cracks in the earth, something began to emerge.

It was massive—a shape that seemed to shift and writhe in the darkness. Enola could barely make it out, but it was huge, covered in scales that shimmered in the light, its eyes glowing like molten lava. The growling had ceased, replaced by a low hiss that echoed through the room.

Enola felt her legs shake beneath her. This was no creature they could face. This was something else entirely.

The tom moved forward, his posture commanding. "It's too late to stop it now," he murmured, more to himself than to anyone else. "All we can do is survive."

Survive. The word seemed to hang in the air, heavy with meaning. Enola felt a chill crawl down her spine. Survive from what?

Suddenly, the massive creature lunged forward, its jaws snapping. Enola's eyes widened as she saw the jagged teeth glint in the dim light. Rook yelped, backing away, but the tom was already moving. He darted forward with a speed Enola hadn't expected, his massive form a blur as he tackled the creature with an almost unnatural force.

Enola's heart pounded as the room erupted into chaos. She wanted to help, wanted to leap into the fray with Rook and the tom, but she was frozen, her mind racing for any kind of strategy. She had no weapons, no experience fighting something like this.

The tom and the creature were locked in a deadly dance, claws and teeth flashing as they fought for dominance. The ground cracked beneath them, and the room shook with every impact. Enola had never seen anything like this before—this wasn't a fight between cats. This was something far more ancient.

"Enola!" Rook shouted, his voice urgent. "Move! We need to get out of here!"

But Enola couldn't tear her eyes away from the struggle before her. The tom's strength was incredible, but even he couldn't seem to hold the creature back for long. It was too strong, too relentless.

"Now!" Rook barked, and this time, Enola didn't hesitate. She turned and bolted toward the door, her legs carrying her faster than she thought possible. She could hear the sounds of the battle behind her—the roar of the creature, the sound of claws scraping against stone—but she didn't stop. She couldn't.

The alleyway outside was dark and narrow, and Enola could hear Rook's rapid footsteps behind her. The sound of the battle had faded, but she could still feel the heavy weight of it pressing on her chest. Whatever that creature was, it wasn't done yet. It was still out there.

They stopped in a clearing, gasping for breath. Enola's mind was a blur of fear and confusion. She hadn't known what to expect when she followed the tom, but this? This was beyond anything she could have imagined.

"What now?" Enola panted, her fur matted with sweat and dirt.

Rook glanced around the dark city, his eyes hard and calculating. "We keep moving," he said, his voice low. "We need to find out more about what we're dealing with. But right now, we can't stay here."

Enola nodded, her heart still pounding in her chest. Whatever had just happened, it was only the beginning. The creature, the tom, the ancient symbol—it was all connected. But how?

As they turned to leave, Enola couldn't shake the feeling that something, someone, was still watching them. Something was waiting for them to make their next move.

And this time, she wasn't sure if they would survive it.

Chapter 8

The city stretched out in front of them, a maze of crumbling streets and abandoned buildings. Enola's paws scraped the pavement as she trotted alongside Rook, the sound of their footsteps muffled by the thick fog that had settled over the town. The air was damp and heavy with the scent of rain, but Enola couldn't shake the feeling that something else lingered—something colder, darker.

They hadn't spoken much since they fled the building. The battle between the tom and the creature had left them all rattled. Enola's mind was swirling with questions—What had they just faced? What was that symbol? And why had the tom been so adamant about them surviving?

Rook, who had been unusually silent, finally broke the quiet. "You're thinking too much," he muttered, glancing sideways at her.

Enola didn't reply at first, unsure how to voice the jumble of thoughts in her mind. "It just doesn't make sense. Why did the tom say 'survive'? What are we really up against?"

Rook's eyes flicked ahead, his expression unreadable. "I don't know, Enola. I don't think even the tom knows. But we're not safe yet. Not by a long shot."

The words hung in the air between them, heavy with meaning. Rook was right; there was something off about everything that had happened. The fight, the creature, the way the tom had acted—it was as if they were caught in the middle of something far beyond their control.

Enola glanced over her shoulder, half-expecting to see the shadow of that creature stalking them from the gloom. But the street behind them was empty, just a dark stretch of pavement lost in the fog. Still, she couldn't shake the sense of being watched, a cold prickle crawling down her spine.

"Do you hear that?" she asked, her voice barely above a whisper.

Rook stopped and tilted his head. "Hear what?"

Enola strained her ears. At first, it was just the sound of the wind rustling through the dead leaves, the faint drip of water from a nearby gutter. But then there was something else, a low, almost imperceptible hum. It vibrated through the ground, like the earth itself was pulsing with energy.

Enola's heart skipped a beat. "That."

Rook's eyes narrowed. He was already moving forward, his steps quickening. "We need to move. Now."

They didn't need to speak anymore. Enola's legs were already in motion, her paws swift and light against the wet pavement. The hum grew louder, more intense, and Enola could feel it in her bones. Something was coming, and it was coming fast.

They darted into an alleyway, the narrow space offering a brief respite from the oppressive darkness of the streets. Rook pressed himself against the wall, ears twitching, his eyes scanning every corner, every shadow. Enola did the same, her tail flicking nervously.

"What is it?" she asked, though she already had a sinking feeling in her stomach.

"I don't know," Rook answered. "But I've never heard anything like it. This is different from the creature we saw earlier. This feels... wrong."

Enola's fur prickled at his words. She could feel it, too. Whatever was causing that hum, it wasn't something natural. It was... unnatural. A cold, alien presence that seemed to stretch across the entire city.

The hum reached a crescendo, the sound vibrating the very air around them, and then—silence. Complete, suffocating silence.

Rook's muscles tensed. "This isn't good."

Before Enola could respond, a shadow shifted in the alleyway ahead. She froze, her breath catching in her throat. It wasn't a cat. It wasn't even something she could fully comprehend. It was a shape—a black void in the shape of a creature, its edges flickering in and out like a broken reflection in water.

Enola's heart raced as the shape moved toward them, its presence distorting the shadows around it. She couldn't tell if it had eyes, if it even had a face. It was just... there, a twisted silhouette in the darkness.

Rook stood in front of her, his body tense and ready to spring. "We need to get out of here," he growled, his voice low but urgent.

The shape paused, as if aware of their presence. Enola's breath caught in her throat as it seemed to stretch, elongating and twisting in ways that defied nature. The shadows it cast danced like living things, creeping along the walls of the alley.

Then, a voice.

It wasn't spoken, not with words. It was more of a thought, a feeling, something that burrowed into Enola's mind and made her skin crawl.

"You can't escape."

The voice was cold, its tone as ancient as the darkness itself. Enola's legs wavered beneath her. She had to fight the urge to flee, but there was nowhere to run. The creature in front of them wasn't something they could outrun.

Rook growled, his voice sharp. "What do you want from us?"

The shape flickered again, its form distorting as it spoke, the words invading Enola's mind like a chill wind. **"Nothing. Yet."**

Enola's heart pounded in her chest, her fear rising to a fever pitch. There was no escape. This was no ordinary creature. This was something far older, far darker than anything she had encountered.

And then, before she could react, the creature lunged.

Chapter 9

Enola's blood ran cold as the creature lunged forward. Time seemed to stretch, each moment suspended in a surreal haze. Her instincts kicked in, her body acting before her mind could process what was happening. She scrambled backward, her claws digging into the slick concrete as she pushed herself away from the creature.

The shadow flickered in and out of existence, moving with a terrifying speed that defied logic. It was as if the very darkness had come alive, and Enola was caught in its grasp.

Rook reacted just as quickly, his body a blur as he darted in front of Enola, blocking her from the creature's path. His growl was deep, guttural, but it was clear that even he was unsure of how to fight something so alien, so unnatural.

"Stay back!" Rook snapped, his eyes never leaving the shifting shape. "This thing isn't like anything we've faced before. It's not just a creature—it's something else entirely."

Enola's heart raced in her chest. The voice it had spoken to her in—cold, emotionless, yet filled with an unnerving presence—still echoed in her mind. **"You can't escape."**

She clenched her paws, feeling a flicker of determination surge through her. "We have to fight it. We can't just let it take us."

Rook shot her a quick glance, his eyes flashing with a mixture of fear and resolve. "We fight, then. But be ready. This won't be easy."

The creature's form shifted once again, and in that instant, Enola saw it more clearly. It wasn't just a shadow—it was a distortion of reality itself, a void that consumed the light around it. Its edges bled into the surrounding darkness, making it hard to focus on any one part of it.

Enola's breath quickened as the creature's shape seemed to solidify, but not in the way she expected. It wasn't a living thing. It was like a ripple in the air itself, a tear in the fabric of the world. The hum had returned, louder now, vibrating the very air they breathed.

Then, without warning, the creature spoke again, its voice invading their minds.

"You are not meant to be here."

The words weren't a command, but a declaration—like a law of nature, an undeniable truth. Enola felt her fur stand on end, her body frozen in place. This was more than a predator. This was something ancient, something that existed beyond time itself.

Rook growled, his tail flicking with irritation. "We'll see about that."

With a sudden burst of movement, he lunged toward the creature, his claws outstretched, ready to strike. But as his paws reached the shadow's edge, they passed straight through it, like he was swiping at smoke. The creature's form rippled and reformed in the blink of an eye, undeterred by the attack.

Enola's stomach sank. This wasn't a physical being. It was something different—something that couldn't be touched, couldn't be fought in the way they knew how.

She had to think fast. Her mind raced for a solution, but there was nothing in her experience that could explain what was happening. It was as if the laws of the world had broken, leaving her and Rook trapped in some twisted version of reality.

The creature shifted again, its form expanding, until it was no longer a single shape but a swirling mass of darkness, like the night sky had bled down into the alley.

"You do not belong here," it repeated, its voice deeper this time, filled with an overwhelming sense of finality. **"I will make you leave."**

Enola's eyes widened. The creature wasn't just threatening them—it was trying to push them out of existence. It was as if their very presence was an aberration, something that needed to be erased.

Her mind scrambled for anything, anything that could give her an edge. She looked around frantically. There had to be something they could use.

Suddenly, her gaze fell on a broken pipe jutting out from the wall of the alley. It was rusted, jagged, but it was there, within reach. If they could disrupt the creature's form—something solid, something real—they might stand a chance.

"Rook!" she hissed, her voice low but urgent. "The pipe!"

Rook glanced over his shoulder, following her gaze. Understanding flickered in his eyes. Without hesitation, he dashed toward the rusted pipe, his paws striking it with all the force he could muster. The pipe groaned under the impact, but it held.

The creature, sensing the disturbance, reacted instantly. Its form writhed in fury, the hum intensifying, the air growing heavy with an oppressive force.

Enola didn't wait for it to strike. She bounded forward, her body low to the ground, moving like a shadow as she reached the pipe. With all her strength, she lunged, sinking her claws into the metal and pulling it free from the wall. The creature howled, its form convulsing violently as the sound of metal scraping against stone filled the alley.

The world seemed to distort further as the creature writhed, its shape flickering wildly. Enola could feel the air thicken around them, the tension unbearable, but the pipe remained in her grasp.

"Now!" Rook shouted, his voice strained.

Enola didn't hesitate. With a surge of adrenaline, she swung the broken pipe, aiming for the heart of the creature's form. The metal collided with the swirling darkness, and in that moment, the world seemed to freeze.

For a second, there was nothing—just the weight of the silence pressing down on them. Then, with a deafening crack, the creature's form shattered, the shadow dissipating like smoke in the wind.

The hum died.

Enola and Rook stood, panting, their bodies shaking with the aftershock of the battle. The alleyway was eerily quiet once more, the darkness around them just... darkness.

But Enola knew this wasn't over. They had only won this battle, not the war.

She turned to Rook, her voice a whisper. "Is it really gone?"

Rook's eyes flicked around, his body still tense. "For now. But it won't be long before something else comes."

And as the last vestiges of the creature's form faded into the fog, Enola couldn't help but wonder—what was this thing, really? And more importantly—what did it want from them?

The answers seemed just beyond reach, like whispers in the dark.

Chapter 10

The air felt heavy, as if the very fabric of reality had been stretched too thin and now struggled to hold itself together. Enola stared at the spot where the creature had vanished, her breath coming in shallow bursts. The pipe she had used to shatter its form lay discarded at her paws, its surface slick with condensation. She wanted to believe it was over, that they had won, but the knot in her stomach told her otherwise.

Rook broke the silence first, his voice low and measured. "We need to move. Now."

Enola glanced at him, her amber eyes wide. "Do you think there are more of them?"

"I don't know," he admitted, his ears swivelling toward the faintest sound. "But whatever that thing was, it wasn't alone. Things like that never are."

The thought sent a shiver down her spine. She nodded, forcing her legs to move even as exhaustion tugged at her body. Together, they slipped deeper into the maze of alleyways, the narrow passages twisting and turning like the coils of a snake. The dim glow of streetlights barely reached these forgotten corners of the city, and every shadow seemed alive with the possibility of danger.

As they moved, Enola's mind raced. The creature had spoken to them, had singled them out with a purpose that felt unnervingly personal. But why? What had she and Rook done to attract its attention? And what did it mean when it said they didn't belong?

"Do you think it was after us specifically?" she asked, breaking the uneasy silence.

Rook hesitated before answering. "I don't know. But it felt... deliberate. Like it knew us."

Enola frowned, her claws scraping against the cracked pavement as she tried to piece together the fragments of her memory. The city had always been dangerous for strays like them, but this—this was something else entirely. It wasn't about territory or survival anymore. It was about something bigger, something she couldn't yet grasp.

The sound of a distant rumble pulled her from her thoughts. At first, she thought it was thunder, but the sky above was clear, the stars twinkling faintly in the polluted haze. The noise grew louder, more distinct—a rhythmic pounding that sent vibrations through the ground beneath their paws.

Rook's ears flattened against his skull. "Something's coming."

Enola's pulse quickened. "Another one of those things?"

"I don't think so." He sniffed the air, his nose twitching. "This smells... different."

The rumble intensified, and soon the source of the noise revealed itself. A pack of stray dogs rounded the corner, their eyes glowing faintly in the dim light. They moved with an unsettling precision, their heads low and their bodies tense. Enola counted at least seven of them, their lean frames scarred from countless fights.

"Strangers in our streets," growled the largest of the pack, a hulking brute with matted fur and a torn ear. His voice was gravelly, each word laced with menace. "You've stirred up trouble tonight."

Rook stepped in front of Enola, his stance protective. "We don't want any trouble."

The lead dog sneered, baring his yellowed teeth. "Too late for that. You've brought the shadows with you. We've seen them. Felt them. And now you're going to pay."

Enola's heart sank. The dogs thought they were responsible for the creature's appearance. She opened her mouth to protest, but Rook shot her a warning glance.

"Look," he said, his voice calm but firm. "We didn't bring that thing here. We fought it, same as you would've."

The dogs didn't seem convinced. They began to circle, their movements slow and predatory. Enola's fur bristled as she pressed closer to Rook, her mind racing for a way out. They were outnumbered, and a fight would only draw more attention—attention they couldn't afford.

"You're lying," snarled a smaller dog with a patchy coat. "We've seen what you've done. You've angered it. Now it's hunting all of us."

"That's not true!" Enola snapped, unable to keep quiet any longer. "We didn't summon it—we barely escaped with our lives!"

The lead dog stopped circling and fixed her with a piercing glare. "Then prove it. Prove you're not the reason the shadows are closing in."

"How?" Rook demanded.

The dog's lips curled into a cruel smile. "The old rail yard. That's where the shadows are strongest. If you're telling the truth, you'll go there and deal with whatever's lurking."

Enola's stomach churned. The old rail yard was a desolate place on the edge of the city, its rusting trains and overgrown tracks a haven for danger. She had avoided it all her life, and now they were being forced to walk straight into it.

"And if we don't?" Rook asked, his voice low and dangerous.

"Then we'll make sure you never walk anywhere again," the lead dog growled.

The threat hung in the air, heavy and unspoken. Enola exchanged a glance with Rook. They didn't have a choice.

"Fine," Rook said at last. "We'll go."

The pack parted to let them pass, their eyes never leaving Enola and Rook as they slipped away. The weight of their stares pressed down on her, but she forced herself to keep moving.

As they left the alley behind, the city seemed to grow quieter, as if holding its breath. The faint hum of the creature's presence still lingered in the back of her mind, a reminder that this was far from over.

"Do you think they're right?" Enola asked softly. "Do you think the shadows are our fault?"

Rook didn't answer right away. When he finally spoke, his voice was heavy. "I don't know. But if there's even a chance they are, we need to find out why."

The rail yard loomed ahead, its skeletal structures silhouetted against the night sky. Enola felt a chill run through her as they approached, the air growing colder with each step. Whatever awaited them in the shadows, she knew one thing for certain: it wouldn't let them leave without a fight.

Chapter 11

The rail yard stretched before them like a graveyard of forgotten machines. Rusted trains sat motionless on their tracks, their hulking forms cloaked in shadows. Grass and weeds had reclaimed much of the space, their wiry stalks swaying gently in the cold night breeze. The only sounds were the faint creaks of metal settling into itself and the distant wail of a siren carried on the wind.

Enola hesitated at the edge of the yard, her paws sinking into the soft earth. Every instinct screamed at her to turn back, to retreat into the relative safety of the city's maze-like alleys. But they couldn't retreat now—not with the dogs watching, not with the questions gnawing at her mind.

Rook stood beside her, his gaze sweeping the area. "We stick together. No matter what."

Enola nodded, drawing strength from his steady presence. "Let's find out what's waiting for us."

They moved cautiously, weaving between the train cars. The smell of rust and oil filled the air, mingling with something else—something faint and acrid that made the fur on Enola's neck stand on end. The rail yard felt alive in a way that was unnatural, like the shadows themselves were watching their every move.

"What do you think the dogs meant about the shadows being strongest here?" Enola whispered.

Rook didn't answer right away. His ears were pricked, his every muscle taut as if waiting for an ambush. Finally, he said, "Whatever it is, we'll know soon enough."

The words had barely left his mouth when a faint hum began to vibrate through the air. Enola froze, her eyes darting around. The sound was eerily familiar, a low, resonant tone that seemed to come from everywhere and nowhere at once.

"It's here," she murmured, her voice trembling.

Rook bared his teeth, his eyes scanning the shadows. "Stay close."

The hum grew louder, pulsing in rhythmic waves that made the air around them feel heavy. Enola's claws scraped against the gravel as she crouched low, her eyes straining to see through the darkness. And then, just as it had in the alley, the shadow appeared.

But this time, it was different. The darkness didn't coalesce into a single form. Instead, it spread like a living fog, creeping across the ground and wrapping itself around the rusted train cars. The edges of the shadow flickered and danced, as if struggling to maintain its shape.

Enola's heart raced. "What is it doing?"

"I don't know," Rook replied, his voice tight. "But it doesn't feel like it's here to talk."

The shadow surged forward, a tendril of darkness lashing out like a whip. Enola barely had time to dodge, the force of the attack sending a spray of gravel into the air. Rook lunged at the tendril, his claws swiping through the darkness, but just as before, his attack passed straight through.

"It's not working!" he growled, frustration evident in his voice.

Enola's mind raced. If the pipe had worked in the alley, maybe they needed something similar here—something physical to disrupt the shadow's form. She scanned the area, her eyes landing on a pile of debris near an overturned train car. Among the twisted metal and broken wood was a shard of glass, its surface gleaming faintly in the dim light.

"Rook! Over there!" she shouted, pointing with her paw.

Rook followed her gaze and nodded. He sprinted toward the debris, his movements quick and precise. Enola stayed behind, her eyes fixed on the shadow as it writhed and twisted. The hum grew louder, more insistent, and she felt a sharp pain in her ears, as if the sound were drilling into her skull.

"Hurry!" she called, her voice strained.

Rook reached the pile and grabbed the shard of glass in his jaws. He turned back toward Enola, his movements cautious as he avoided cutting himself on the sharp edges. The shadow seemed to sense his intentions and lashed out again, its tendrils whipping through the air with deadly precision.

Enola darted forward, placing herself between Rook and the shadow. She leaped and twisted, her claws raking against the ground as she dodged the tendrils. Each movement was instinctual, her body acting on pure adrenaline. She could hear Rook's paws pounding against the gravel as he closed the distance.

"I've got it!" he shouted around the shard.

Enola turned just in time to see him swing the glass shard toward the shadow. The moment it made contact, the darkness recoiled, a piercing screech echoing through the rail yard. The hum faltered, the oppressive weight in the air lifting slightly.

"It's working!" Enola exclaimed, hope surging through her.

Rook didn't stop. He struck again and again, each blow causing the shadow to shrink and falter. The tendrils retracted, and the fog-like mass began to dissipate, its edges fraying like smoke caught in the wind.

But then, just as it seemed they were gaining the upper hand, the shadow changed. It condensed suddenly, pulling itself into a single, concentrated form. It hovered in the air, its shape shifting and flickering, before surging forward with terrifying speed.

"Rook, look out!" Enola screamed.

Rook jumped to the side, the shadow missing him by a hair's breadth. It collided with the ground, sending a shockwave that rattled the train cars and knocked Enola off her paws. She scrambled to her feet, her vision swimming.

The shadow reared up, its form towering over them. For the first time, Enola felt true fear—not just for herself, but for Rook. They were outmatched. The shard of glass had worked for a moment, but it wasn't enough. They needed something stronger, something permanent.

"Enola!" Rook's voice snapped her out of her thoughts. "We need to fall back!"

She hesitated, her instincts screaming at her to fight, to stand her ground. But as the shadow loomed closer, she knew he was right. They couldn't win this fight—not here, not now.

"Go!" she shouted, turning and sprinting toward the edge of the yard.

Rook was right behind her, the sound of his paws pounding against the gravel a steady rhythm that matched her own. The shadow roared, a deep, guttural sound that seemed to shake the very ground beneath them. Enola didn't look back. She couldn't.

As they reached the edge of the yard, the hum faded, replaced by an eerie silence. Enola slowed to a stop, her chest heaving as she tried to catch her breath. Rook collapsed beside her, the shard of glass still clutched in his jaws.

"We... we have to find out what that thing is," Enola said between gasps.

Rook nodded, his eyes dark. "And we need help. This isn't something we can face alone."

Enola's gaze drifted back toward the rail yard. The shadows had receded, but she knew they hadn't seen the last of them. Whatever this was, it wasn't just their fight anymore. It was something far bigger, and it was only just beginning.

Chapter 12

The night clung to them like a heavy shroud as Enola and Rook crept away from the rail yard. Their paws were silent against the cracked pavement, but their hearts hammered loud enough to drown out the quiet. The confrontation with the shadow still echoed in their minds, each flicker of movement in the dark setting their nerves on edge.

"We can't go back there," Rook said finally, his voice breaking the oppressive silence. "Not until we know what we're dealing with."

Enola nodded, though her thoughts were far from settled. "That thing... it's not just an enemy, Rook. It's something bigger—something we can't outrun forever."

The weight of her words settled between them, but neither offered a solution. The glass shard Rook carried glinted faintly in the moonlight, a fragile reminder of their small victory. But Enola knew it wasn't enough. They needed more than makeshift weapons—they needed answers.

As they padded toward the outskirts of the city, the air grew colder, and the silence deepened. The buildings here were skeletal remains of a world long abandoned, their windows hollow and their walls crumbling. It was a place forgotten by time, a fitting refuge for fugitives of the unknown.

Rook broke the silence again. "The dogs mentioned the shadows being strongest there. Do you think they know more than they're letting on?"

Enola hesitated. The dogs' warning had been cryptic, but there had been something in their tone—fear, maybe, or understanding—that hinted at deeper knowledge. "If they do, we'll need to find out. But I doubt they'll tell us willingly."

Rook growled softly, his frustration evident. "Then we make them talk. If they've faced this thing before, they might know how to stop it."

Enola frowned but didn't argue. The tension between them was palpable, but it wasn't directed at each other—it was the shadow, the hum, the unknown that had frayed their nerves to the breaking point.

Ahead, the ruins of an old warehouse loomed, its rusted doors hanging ajar. Enola slowed her pace, her eyes scanning the area for movement. "We'll rest here for now," she said. "We need to regroup before we decide our next move."

Rook nodded, his tail flicking as he followed her inside. The air was stale and musty, but it offered shelter from the biting wind. They found a corner where the walls were still intact and settled down, their bodies pressed against the cold concrete.

For a while, neither spoke. The weight of the night's events hung heavy over them, each lost in their own thoughts. Enola's mind kept circling back to the shadow, its unnatural presence, and the way it had spoken to them—not with words, but with something deeper, something that touched the very core of her being.

"We can't keep running," she said finally, breaking the silence. "If we do, it'll just keep coming for us. And for others."

Rook looked at her, his expression grim. "Then what do you suggest? We don't even know what it is, let alone how to stop it."

Enola's ears flicked back, frustration bubbling beneath the surface. "We start by finding someone who does. The dogs, maybe. Or the cats at the outskirts. Someone has to know something."

Rook's gaze softened, and he let out a sigh. "Alright. But we move carefully. We can't afford to make mistakes."

Enola nodded, grateful for his steady presence. Together, they would face whatever came next.

As the first light of dawn began to seep through the cracks in the warehouse walls, Enola felt a glimmer of hope. The shadows might be strong, but so were they. And if they could uncover the truth, maybe—just maybe—they could put an end to the darkness once and for all.

Chapter 13

The rising sun painted the ruined warehouse in muted golds and browns, chasing away the chill of the night but doing little to ease the tension hanging between Enola and Rook. As the first rays crept through the cracks in the walls, Rook stirred from his place against the concrete, the glass shard still within reach.

Enola had been awake for hours, her thoughts spinning in endless loops. Every time she closed her eyes, the shadow surged back into her mind: its unnatural movement, the pulsing hum, the cold sense of despair that clung to it. They'd survived by luck—nothing more. And luck wasn't a strategy.

Rook stretched, shaking off the stiffness from the hard floor. "You didn't sleep," he said without looking at her.

"I couldn't." Enola stood, shaking out her fur. "Too much to think about."

He nodded, his expression unreadable. "We need a plan."

Enola agreed but didn't respond immediately. She padded toward the warehouse's gaping doorway, her paws crunching softly against debris. Beyond the threshold, the city stretched out like a wounded beast, its crumbling towers and tangled alleys concealing more questions than answers. Somewhere out there were the dogs—keepers of cryptic warnings—and maybe others who had encountered the shadow and lived to tell about it.

"We'll go back to the dogs," Enola said finally, turning to face Rook. "We need to know what they know. Even if they don't want to talk, we'll make them."

Rook's ears twitched. "And if they don't know anything useful?"

Enola hesitated, the weight of the uncertainty settling on her shoulders. "Then we'll find someone who does. There are others—cats on the outskirts, scavengers in the old tunnels. Someone has to have answers."

Rook didn't argue. Instead, he stepped past her and toward the city. "Let's get moving. The longer we wait, the stronger that thing gets."

They set out in silence, their steps careful and measured. The morning light brought no comfort; instead, it revealed the city's scars in stark detail. Abandoned cars rusted in the streets, their windows shattered and frames consumed by time. Ivy and weeds clawed at the remnants of human construction, nature slowly reclaiming what had been taken from it.

As they approached the city's heart, the familiar sounds of distant movement reached their ears. Paws against pavement, low growls, and hushed voices. Enola's ears perked, her body tensing as she signalled for Rook to stop.

"They're close," she whispered.

Rook nodded, his muscles taut as they crept forward, staying low to the ground. The sounds grew louder, and soon, the source came into view: three dogs huddled around a patch of sunlight that broke through the city's jagged skyline. They were large and lean, their fur marked with scars that told of countless battles. Their postures were tense, their voices sharp with urgency.

"—told you it's spreading," one of them growled. "The shadows won't stop until they've swallowed everything."

"And what do you suggest we do?" another snapped. "March into its lair and demand it leave? We've tried fighting it. We've tried running. It doesn't matter."

The third dog, a wiry creature with a patch of fur missing from his flank, let out a low snarl. "Then we warn the others. At least give them a chance to run before it's too late."

Enola exchanged a glance with Rook. These dogs knew something—more than they'd let on during their last encounter. And from the sound of it, they were just as desperate to stop the shadow as she was.

"Let me handle this," Enola murmured, stepping forward.

The dogs' heads snapped toward her as she emerged from the shadows, their growls rumbling low in their throats. Rook followed close behind, his presence a silent warning.

"You again," the wiry dog snarled. "Didn't you get the message last time? Stay out of it."

"We can't," Enola said firmly. "That thing attacked us last night. We barely made it out alive. And from the sound of it, you're not doing much better."

The dogs exchanged wary glances but didn't respond.

"We're not here to fight," Enola continued, taking a cautious step closer. "We need information. Anything you know about the shadow—what it is, where it came from, how to stop it."

The largest dog bared his teeth, his eyes narrowing. "And what makes you think we'd tell you?"

"Because we're on the same side," Rook said, his voice calm but edged with steel. "If we don't work together, none of us will survive this."

For a moment, silence hung in the air, thick with tension. Then, the wiry dog let out a sharp bark of laughter, though there was no humour in it.

"Same side, huh?" he said. "Funny, coming from a couple of strays who don't even know what they're up against."

"Then tell us," Enola pressed. "Help us understand."

The wiry dog's eyes darkened, and his voice dropped to a low growl. "The shadow isn't just some monster. It's... old. Older than the city, older than us. And it's hungry. It feeds on fear, on despair. Every time it takes a life, it grows stronger. And once it's strong enough..." He trailed off, his gaze distant.

"Once it's strong enough, what?" Rook demanded.

The dog hesitated, his jaw working as if struggling with the weight of his words. Finally, he said, "Once it's strong enough, it'll consume everything. Not just the city. Everything."

The words sent a chill down Enola's spine, but she refused to let the fear take hold. "How do we stop it?"

The largest dog let out a bitter laugh. "You don't. You run. And even then, it might not be enough."

Enola squared her shoulders, her voice steady. "Running isn't an option. Not for us. So unless you want to sit back and watch the world burn, you'll tell us what you know."

The dogs exchanged another glance, their expressions conflicted. Finally, the wiry dog sighed and nodded.

"There's a place," he said. "A place where it all started. The heart of the city. If there's any way to stop it, that's where you'll find it. But getting there..." He shook his head. "You won't make it out alive."

Enola's gaze hardened. "We'll see about that."

Chapter 14

The dogs' warning echoed in Enola's mind as she and Rook moved deeper into the ruins of the city, the words sinking into her bones. The heart of the city. Where it all started. If there was any hope of stopping the shadow, it would be there. But their chances of making it through the heart of the city alive were slim, and they both knew it.

The wiry dog's bitter words replayed over and over in Enola's head. *You won't make it out alive.* But Enola couldn't afford to let that stop her. The shadow was already spreading, and every passing moment brought them closer to losing everything.

"We have to try, Rook," she said, her voice firm despite the doubt gnawing at her. "If there's even a chance of stopping this, we can't waste it."

Rook didn't argue. His expression remained unreadable as they continued their journey toward the heart of the city. The streets were quieter now, the remnants of the old world around them lying in ruin. The fog had not lifted, and the air was thick with unease. It felt like the city was holding its breath, waiting for something.

Enola scanned their surroundings, every shadow seeming to move and shift, every alleyway hiding some unseen threat. She couldn't shake the feeling that they were being watched.

"Keep your eyes open," she murmured to Rook.

He nodded, his eyes darting from one side of the street to the other. "We'll make it. We just need to keep moving."

As they pressed on, the buildings grew taller, more imposing, until the streets seemed to narrow, forcing them into the shadow of the massive structures. It was in these narrow, labyrinthine alleys that Enola felt the full weight of the city's desolation. The air was thick with the scent of decay, and every crack in the concrete seemed to pulse with the energy of something ancient, something wrong.

They passed through a long-forgotten market square, where the remnants of old stalls lay shattered in the street, and crumbling signs swung in the breeze. The city's heart was close.

But so was something else.

Suddenly, a low, menacing growl broke the silence, followed by the sharp sound of paws skittering against the ground.

Enola's fur stood on end as she spun around, her heart pounding in her chest. A pack of creatures—dark shapes with glowing eyes—emerged from the shadows. Their movements were fluid, like the very darkness around them, and their forms seemed to flicker in and out of existence.

Rook was by her side in an instant, his hackles raised. "It's them," he muttered, his voice tight. "The shadow's followers. The ones that protect it."

Enola didn't hesitate. "We can't fight them all. We need to keep moving."

But before they could retreat, one of the creatures lunged, its claws slashing through the air. Enola leapt back, narrowly avoiding the strike. The creature hissed, its form rippling as it prepared for another attack.

"We need a way out," Rook growled, his teeth bared.

Enola scanned the area frantically. They were surrounded. There was no clear path to escape. But then she spotted something—a narrow passageway between two buildings, barely wide enough for them to squeeze through.

"That way!" she shouted, darting toward the gap.

Rook was right behind her, his movements swift and practiced. But the creatures weren't far behind. Their growls grew louder, more insistent as they closed in. Enola felt a surge of panic rise in her chest. They couldn't outrun them forever.

The passageway was narrow, and Enola had to squeeze through tightly, her sides brushing against the crumbling stone walls. Behind her, Rook did the same, his fur brushing against hers. The growls of the shadow's followers were close, their claws scraping against the walls as they pursued.

And then—just as they reached the end of the passage, a figure appeared ahead of them.

It was a dog, standing in the shadow of a broken building. His fur was matted and worn, his eyes wild with fear.

"Go! Now!" he shouted, waving them toward him. "I know the way!"

Without thinking, Enola bolted toward the figure, Rook following closely behind. The dog turned, leading them through a series of twisting alleys, the shadow's followers still hot on their heels.

They finally reached a small, hidden doorway, barely noticeable against the crumbling stone. The dog pushed it open, ushering them inside.

Enola stumbled into the darkness beyond, panting. "Who are you?" she demanded, her voice hoarse.

The dog's eyes gleamed with a mix of fear and determination. "My name's Aros. I'm one of the few who knows how to survive in this city. And right now, you need all the help you can get."

Rook's eyes narrowed. "What do you want from us?"

Aros stepped back, his gaze flicking to the door they had just entered. "What I want is to stop the shadow. But I can't do it alone. I've seen what it's capable of, and I've been running from it for longer than I care to admit." He glanced at Enola, his voice steady. "You're not the only ones who've felt its hunger."

Enola swallowed, her mind racing. This was it. They had a chance to stop the shadow. But they weren't out of danger yet.

Aros stepped forward. "The heart of the city—where it all began—is still our best chance. But you're not the only ones heading there. And you'll need more than just courage to survive the path ahead."

Enola's heart skipped a beat. "What do you mean?"

Aros hesitated, his gaze flicking to the door. "You're not the only ones searching for answers. There are others out there, and some of them are not what they seem."

Before Enola could respond, the door shuddered.

Chapter 15

The door shuddered again, the sound of claws scraping against stone sending a cold chill down Enola's spine. She turned quickly to Aros, her breath quickening as she realized the gravity of their situation.

"How many are there?" she asked urgently, her eyes scanning the dimly lit room.

Aros didn't answer right away. His face was drawn, his eyes flicking between the door and Enola. "More than I'd like to admit," he said grimly. "The shadow's followers aren't just a pack—they're a force. And there's no escaping them once they've marked you."

Enola's mind raced. If they didn't get out of here soon, they'd be trapped. But even more pressing was what Aros had said—others were searching for the heart of the city, too. And not all of them could be trusted.

"We need to move," Rook muttered, his low growl rising in his throat. "We can't fight them all."

Aros nodded. "I know a way through the old tunnels. It's dangerous, but it's the only way to the heart that doesn't go through the open city. The shadow's followers are less likely to patrol that route, but it's a risk, just the same."

Enola hesitated, her mind still grappling with the words that Aros had dropped. *Others*. Who else would be out there? Were they allies or enemies? It was hard to trust anyone in this desolate world, especially with the shadow growing stronger with every passing minute.

"Lead the way," Enola said, her voice steady despite the unease bubbling inside her. There was no time to waste.

Aros led them through a narrow corridor that twisted and turned through the heart of the ruins. The air was stale and damp, and the walls seemed to close in around them as they descended into the dark tunnels beneath the city. The only sounds were their breathing and the occasional distant drip of water.

"How do you know about these tunnels?" Rook asked, his voice echoing in the stillness.

Aros didn't answer right away, his footfalls soft but steady. "I've been here a long time. Longer than you'd believe. These tunnels used to be part of the city's old transport system. Before everything went wrong, before the shadow." His voice dropped to a low murmur. "There are things down here. Things that have been hiding for years."

Enola couldn't help but feel the weight of his words. What could possibly be worse than the shadow itself? The thought gnawed at her as they continued deeper into the earth.

After what felt like hours, they reached a small cavern. Aros gestured for them to stop. "This is where we part ways," he said, his face grim. "You'll need to take the left path. It's the quickest way to the heart of the city. But be careful. It's not just the shadow's followers you'll need to worry about. There are... others down there."

Enola frowned. "What do you mean, 'others'?"

Aros' eyes flickered with something unreadable. "Not all creatures down here are enemies. But they don't take kindly to strangers. And the closer you get to the heart, the more dangerous things become."

Rook stepped forward, his voice low and cautious. "What happens if we don't follow your advice?"

Aros looked away, his lips curling into a bitter smile. "Then you'll be on your own. But I wouldn't recommend it."

Enola was about to speak when the distant sound of heavy footsteps echoed through the tunnel. Someone, or something, was coming.

"Go!" Aros barked, his eyes wide. "Hurry!"

Without another word, Enola turned and ran, Rook at her heels. The sound of footsteps grew louder, and the air seemed to thicken with dread. As they rounded a corner, Enola's heart lurched.

The tunnel ahead had collapsed.

It wasn't a small cave-in; it was a massive block of stone and debris, effectively sealing off their route. Panic surged in Enola's chest, and she skidded to a halt. "We're trapped!"

Rook was right behind her, his muscles tense as he surveyed their options. "We can't go back now. The shadow's followers are too close."

Enola's mind raced. Aros had said to take the left path, but now that was impossible. They needed another way out.

"Over here," she said urgently, spotting a narrow gap between the rocks. It was tight, but it might just be enough for them to squeeze through.

Rook didn't hesitate. He shoved against the debris, his strong frame forcing the stones to shift just enough to make a small opening. Enola pushed forward, her heart hammering as she wriggled through the gap.

On the other side, the air was fresher, but the tunnel seemed even darker. A cold breeze brushed her fur, carrying with it a faint scent of something... unfamiliar.

"We're close," Rook murmured, his voice full of tension.

They pressed on, moving through the tight space until the tunnel widened into a cavern. The walls here were covered in strange markings—symbols Enola didn't recognize. They glowed faintly, pulsing like a heartbeat.

"What is this place?" Enola whispered.

Rook's ears twitched. "No idea. But I've never seen anything like it."

Before Enola could respond, a shadow moved in the distance.

Chapter 16

The figure in the shadows moved closer, its form shifting in and out of the dim light cast by the strange glowing symbols. Enola's heart skipped a beat. She instinctively drew closer to Rook, her muscles tense as she tried to make sense of what was before her. The air grew heavier, thick with a presence that was both unsettling and powerful.

The figure stepped into the faint light, revealing a tall, thin creature draped in tattered, dark robes. Its face was obscured by a hood, but its eyes—bright, cold, and unsettling—glowed like twin embers in the dark. They seemed to pierce through the darkness, locking onto Enola with an intensity that made her skin crawl.

"Who are you?" Rook growled, his fur bristling as he positioned himself protectively in front of Enola.

The creature didn't respond right away. Instead, it tilted its head slightly, as though studying them. Then, its voice—a soft whisper like the rustling of dry leaves—drifted through the air.

"You are not supposed to be here," it said, its tone both a warning and a question.

Enola's claws dug into the stone beneath her paws. "We're looking for answers," she said, trying to keep her voice steady despite the growing unease. "We need to know about the shadow. The heart of the city. How to stop it."

The figure's glowing eyes seemed to narrow. "You seek to stop it?" The voice was incredulous, as if the very idea was laughable. "The shadow cannot be stopped. It is a force older than the city itself, older than anything you can comprehend."

Enola's stomach tightened. "We have to try," she said, her voice firm despite the creature's ominous words.

For a long moment, the figure remained silent, its glowing eyes studying them both. Then, without warning, it stepped forward, closing the distance between them in a single, fluid motion. Enola flinched but held her ground.

"Then you are fools," the figure said, its voice suddenly cold and harsh. "But if you are determined, I can offer you guidance." The air around them seemed to grow colder, and Enola's breath formed small clouds in the space between them.

"Why help us?" Rook asked, his voice suspicious. "What's in it for you?"

The figure's hooded face tilted upward, revealing nothing but shadows. "Because you are not the first to come. Others have tried before you. All have failed." It paused, as if savouring the weight of the words. "But you, you are different. You are the last hope for this city. For what remains of it."

Enola felt a flicker of hope rise within her, but it was quickly dampened by a deeper sense of foreboding. "What do you want in exchange?" she asked, her voice steady despite the swirling mix of emotions inside her.

The figure seemed to consider the question for a moment before it spoke again, its voice quieter now, almost mournful.

"I want nothing," it said. "But you will need to be prepared for what lies ahead. The path you seek is fraught with dangers far worse than what you have already faced. The shadow feeds on fear, on despair. It will twist your mind, you very will to survive. If you wish to stand a chance, you must be strong—stronger than you've ever been."

Enola's gaze met Rook's, and for a brief moment, they shared a silent understanding. They had already seen the shadow's effects firsthand, and they knew that if they didn't find a way to stop it soon, the city—maybe the world—would be consumed by it.

The figure extended one long, skeletal hand toward them. "Come, then," it said, its voice now thick with finality. "Follow me. The heart of the city awaits."

Without waiting for a response, it turned and began to walk deeper into the cavern, its long, flowing robes trailing behind it like a shadow itself. Enola hesitated for only a moment before nodding to Rook.

"We don't have much choice," she said softly, though doubt flickered in her eyes.

Rook's low growl rumbled in his chest, but he followed her without argument. "I don't like it," he muttered, his voice laced with suspicion. "Something about that thing feels wrong."

"I know," Enola replied, her voice tinged with unease. "But right now, it's our only lead."

They moved quickly, keeping close to the figure as it led them through the twisting tunnels. The path grew narrower, the air thicker with the scent of damp stone and decay. Every step felt heavier, and the silence pressed in around them like a weight.

Eventually, they reached a vast chamber, the size of a small city block. The ceiling was lost in darkness above them, and the walls were lined with more of the eerie glowing symbols. The floor was uneven, cracked in places, and littered with debris. At the far end of the chamber stood a massive stone door, its surface covered in intricate carvings that seemed to shimmer faintly in the dark.

"This is it," the figure said, its voice echoing in the cavern. "The heart of the city."

Enola took a deep breath, her heart pounding in her chest. Whatever lay beyond this door, it was the answer they had been searching for. But she couldn't shake the feeling that they were walking straight into the mouth of a trap.

The figure approached the door and pressed a hand to the cold stone surface. The carvings on the door began to glow brighter, pulsing with a rhythmic energy. Slowly, the massive door began to creak open, revealing a blinding light beyond.

Enola squinted, her eyes adjusting to the sudden brightness. She could feel the power radiating from within, an overwhelming force that sent a chill through her fur.

"Are you ready?" Rook asked, his voice low and tense. "Once we step through, there's no turning back."

Enola nodded, her resolve hardening. "We have to stop this. For everyone."

The figure stepped aside, gesturing toward the opening. "Then go," it whispered. "But beware—the shadow is always watching."

Enola and Rook exchanged one final glance before stepping forward into the blinding light. As the door closed behind them, the air seemed to hum with energy. The weight of what they were about to face pressed down on them, but there was no turning back now.

Suddenly, the ground beneath their paws shifted. A deep, guttural growl rumbled from the darkness ahead.

Chapter 17

The growl echoed through the chamber, reverberating off the walls and filling the air with a palpable sense of dread. Enola and Rook froze in place, their bodies tense, every muscle screaming for them to run, but they stayed rooted to the spot. The light that had once been blinding now seemed to flicker, casting long, unnerving shadows that twisted and danced across the cracked floor.

The growl came again, louder this time, followed by the sound of something heavy scraping against stone. Enola's fur stood on end. Whatever was in the darkness, it was big—and it was moving closer.

"Stay sharp," Rook whispered, his voice barely audible over the rising hum in the air.

They crept forward cautiously, every step measured, the weight of the unknown pressing down on them. The light from the stone door flickered again, casting harsh shadows that made the room feel even larger and more claustrophobic. They passed ancient, worn-out statues standing like silent sentinels, their faces half-erased by time.

Enola could hear the sounds of something breathing, low and ragged, just beyond their line of sight. She motioned for Rook to stop and crouch low beside her.

"I don't like this," Enola muttered, her breath shallow. "This place... it feels like we've walked into the heart of the shadow itself."

Rook didn't answer immediately, his eyes scanning the darkness ahead. His growl was barely audible when he finally spoke. "Whatever it is, it's too quiet. I don't trust it."

They continued forward, but each step felt heavier than the last. The cavern seemed to stretch endlessly, and yet they were no closer to the source of the growling. Enola's heart thudded in her chest, a rhythm that matched the growing intensity of the hum in the air.

Suddenly, the scraping noise stopped.

A sharp, unnatural silence descended over them.

Enola's ears twitched. Something wasn't right.

Before she could say anything, a flash of movement broke the stillness. A shadow darted across the chamber, quick and fluid, too fast for her to follow with her eyes. Her claws scraped the stone as she spun to face the direction of the movement, but there was nothing. Only darkness.

Then came the whisper.

It wasn't a voice—it was more of a sensation. A cold pressure in her mind, a brush of words that she could almost feel, like a breath against her fur.

You're too late.

Enola's blood ran cold. Her breath caught in her throat. She had heard those words before—whispers from the shadows in the alley, the oppressive feeling of being watched.

Rook's fur bristled beside her. "Did you hear that?"

She nodded, unable to form words. Something—or someone—was here, watching them, waiting for them to make the first move.

Then, without warning, the lights flickered again, and the growl returned. This time it was louder, more menacing. It came from above.

Enola looked up just in time to see a massive, dark shape descending from the ceiling, its form enormous and unsettling. The creature—whatever it was—had limbs like twisted branches, its body made of dark, shifting tendrils that seemed to writhe and coil in the air.

It was the shadow itself.

Rook lunged forward with a roar, his claws unsheathing as he swiped at the creature. But his claws met nothing but air as the shadow writhed and shifted, slipping through his attack as if it were made of smoke. The growl grew deeper, vibrating the ground beneath them, and Enola felt the air grow colder still, a coldness that seemed to seep into her very bones.

The shadow reared back, and for a moment, Enola saw its form more clearly—its long, clawed limbs, its faceless, amorphous body, its eyes—eyes like the burning embers of a dying fire, glowing with a hunger that sent a tremor through her body.

"Run!" Enola shouted, her voice breaking through the terror that threatened to paralyze her.

But as she turned, she saw that the path they had entered through had vanished. The stone door was no longer there. There was only an endless expanse of darkness ahead, the growls and the sinister whispers closing in from all sides.

The shadow advanced on them again, its tendrils curling toward Rook with terrifying speed. He barely managed to dodge one swipe, but his movements were slow—too slow. Enola's heart raced as she watched him struggle.

"Rook!" she cried, but the sound of her voice was drowned out by the deafening growl of the creature.

Suddenly, the shadow shifted again, and something changed in the air. It was as though the room itself had come alive—cracks appeared in the stone floor, and the eerie symbols on the walls flared with a sickly glow. The temperature dropped even further, and a dark, oppressive force seemed to pulse in the air, pushing against Enola and Rook.

Enola's claws dug into the ground, her mind racing for any idea, any hope. She needed to act fast—there was no way they could face this thing without a plan.

Then, out of nowhere, a sharp, high-pitched sound split the air—a sound like the screech of metal being torn apart. The shadow shrieked, its form writhing and contorting as though it were being torn apart by some invisible force.

The light around them flared briefly, and in the moment of confusion, Enola caught a glimpse of something—or someone—standing in the distance. It was barely visible, but its presence was undeniable.

A figure cloaked in darkness, much like the shadow itself, but different. There was a familiarity in the figure's shape that made Enola's breath hitch.

She couldn't see its face, but the figure was standing still, watching the shadow as it fought against the unknown force. The growling ceased, replaced by the sound of something breathing—a slow, deliberate inhale, as if the figure itself were waiting for something.

"Who are you?" Enola breathed, her voice hoarse.

But before the figure could answer, the shadow roared, and in a burst of energy, it surged forward toward the figure—toward Enola and Rook.

Chapter 18

The air crackled with tension, the heartbeat of the city pulsing beneath their paws. Enola's chest tightened as she felt the invisible force pulling her forward, drawing her toward the cloaked figure. Her instincts screamed at her to run, to fight back, but the pull was too strong, too undeniable. It was as if the very ground beneath her feet was bending to its will.

Rook, ever vigilant, didn't hesitate. With a low growl, he darted in front of Enola, his body a shield between her and the approaching shadow. His claws scraped against the floor as he prepared for another strike, his muscles coiled, ready for anything.

But the shadow didn't go for him.

Instead, it surged toward Enola, its tendrils slashing the air, dark energy trailing in its wake. The sound of its growl was deafening, vibrating through her chest. The figure—whoever it was—stood still, its presence radiating a calm that felt almost unnatural in the chaos of the moment.

The shadow closed the distance with terrifying speed, and for a split second, Enola thought it was too late. Its claws reached for her, the dark tendrils swirling, intent on wrapping around her like a vice.

But then, the figure moved.

It wasn't a swift motion—it was subtle, deliberate. A single hand raised, fingers outstretched, as if to stop time itself. And just like that, the shadow faltered. Its tendrils jerked and twisted, as if trying to break free from the figure's unseen grip.

A sharp, painful silence followed, and Enola felt the oppressive force of the shadow loosen, just enough for her to breathe again.

"Stay back," the figure's voice broke through the silence—a low, rasping whisper that seemed to echo directly in Enola's mind. "I've been waiting for you."

Enola's heart raced. She had no idea who this figure was or why they were here, but the urgency in their voice left no room for questions. Without thinking, Enola took a step back, her body still tingling from the eerie sensation of the figure's presence.

Rook remained tense, his muscles taut as he growled low under his breath. "What are you?" he demanded, but his voice lacked the conviction it usually held. Even he was uncertain in the face of this mysterious force.

The figure didn't answer right away. Instead, it turned its head slightly, the hood of its cloak shifting just enough for Enola to glimpse a pair of glowing eyes, an amber fire burning within. The figure's face was obscured, but the eyes spoke volumes—there was a deep sadness within them, and something else: a recognition. As if it had seen Enola before, though she didn't remember it.

"The shadow is not what you think it is," the figure said, its voice like the wind through cracked stone. "It's not a monster. It's a memory—one that refuses to fade, one that feeds on despair and fear."

Enola blinked, confusion clouding her mind. "What do you mean? How could something like this be a memory?"

The figure hesitated, as if weighing its words carefully. Then, in a voice that was almost too quiet to hear, it said, "The shadow is born of the city's past. A past long buried, a past filled with secrets. It is a remnant of the ones who came before you, before all of us. It's been waiting for someone to awaken it—someone to make it whole again."

Rook growled again, this time louder, frustration building. "Why are you telling us this? What do you want from us?"

The figure's gaze flickered to Rook, then back to Enola. There was something in the way it looked at her—a flicker of something old, something that felt like fate.

"I want nothing from you," it said, its tone softer now. "I've seen your journey, seen your struggle. But you cannot stop the shadow by fighting it directly. That is its power—to make you fear it, to break you from the inside out. You must understand it."

Enola's breath caught. The shadow was more than just a creature of the dark. It was something deeper, tied to the city's very soul, to the forgotten history beneath its cracked surface.

"How do we stop it?" Enola's voice trembled with the weight of the question, her mind racing with the possibilities. Was it possible to even stop something so ancient, so deeply embedded in the world's fabric?

The figure's eyes dimmed, as if they, too, carried the burden of that knowledge. "You must face the past. The heart of the city, where the shadow began, is the only place where it can be undone. But..."

The figure paused, and for the first time, there was a trace of uncertainty in its voice. "There is another way—a more dangerous way. But it requires a sacrifice. A choice."

Enola's pulse quickened. "A sacrifice? What do you mean? What choice?"

The figure took a step forward, its movements unnervingly smooth, as if it were one with the very air around it. "You must choose to let the past die. Or, if you choose wrong, the shadow will consume everything—everything you've fought for, everything you care about."

The room seemed to tighten around her, the shadow twitching and jerking as it tried to break free of its invisible binds. Enola's heart pounded in her chest. Was there truly a way to stop this nightmare? Could she really let go of everything that tied her to this place—her past, her memories, everything that made her who she was?

The figure's voice dropped to a whisper, barely audible against the deafening growl of the shadow, "The choice lies with you. And if you fail, it will be the end of all."

Enola stepped forward, her mind a whirlwind. The future seemed to stretch out before her—a thousand possibilities, none of them clear, none of them safe. Her claws dug into the ground, the pressure of the moment bearing down on her.

Then, in the instant before she could speak, the shadow broke free.

It surged forward, more powerful than ever, its tendrils whirling through the air with unrelenting speed.

Chapter 19

The air crackled with tension, the heartbeat of the city pulsing beneath their paws. Enola's chest tightened as she felt the invisible force pulling her forward, drawing her toward the cloaked figure. Her instincts screamed at her to run, to fight back, but the pull was too strong, too undeniable. It was as if the very ground beneath her feet was bending to its will.

Rook, ever vigilant, didn't hesitate. With a low growl, he darted in front of Enola, his body a shield between her and the approaching shadow. His claws scraped against the floor as he prepared for another strike, his muscles coiled, ready for anything.

But the shadow didn't go for him.

Instead, it surged toward Enola, its tendrils slashing the air, dark energy trailing in its wake. The sound of its growl was deafening, vibrating through her chest. The figure—whoever it was—stood still, its presence radiating a calm that felt almost unnatural in the chaos of the moment.

The shadow closed the distance with terrifying speed, and for a split second, Enola thought it was too late. Its claws reached for her, the dark tendrils swirling, intent on wrapping around her like a vice.

But then, the figure moved.

It wasn't a swift motion—it was subtle, deliberate. A single hand raised, fingers outstretched, as if to stop time itself. And just like that, the shadow faltered. Its tendrils jerked and twisted, as if trying to break free from the figure's unseen grip.

A sharp, painful silence followed, and Enola felt the oppressive force of the shadow loosen, just enough for her to breathe again.

"Stay back," the figure's voice broke through the silence—a low, rasping whisper that seemed to echo directly in Enola's mind. "I've been waiting for you."

Enola's heart raced. She had no idea who this figure was or why they were here, but the urgency in their voice left no room for questions. Without thinking, Enola took a step back, her body still tingling from the eerie sensation of the figure's presence.

Rook remained tense, his muscles taut as he growled low under his breath. "What are you?" he demanded, but his voice lacked the conviction it usually held. Even he was uncertain in the face of this mysterious force.

The figure didn't answer right away. Instead, it turned its head slightly, the hood of its cloak shifting just enough for Enola to glimpse a pair of glowing eyes, an amber fire burning within. The figure's face was obscured, but the eyes spoke volumes—there was a deep sadness within them, and something else: a recognition. As if it had seen Enola before, though she didn't remember it.

"The shadow is not what you think it is," the figure said, its voice like the wind through cracked stone. "It's not a monster. It's a memory—one that refuses to fade, one that feeds on despair and fear."

Enola blinked, confusion clouding her mind. "What do you mean? How could something like this be a memory?"

The figure hesitated, as if weighing its words carefully. Then, in a voice that was almost too quiet to hear, it said, "The shadow is born of the city's past. A past long buried, a past filled with secrets. It is a remnant of the ones who came before you, before all of us. It's been waiting for someone to awaken it—someone to make it whole again."

Rook growled again, this time louder, frustration building. "Why are you telling us this? What do you want from us?"

The figure's gaze flickered to Rook, then back to Enola. There was something in the way it looked at her—a flicker of something old, something that felt like fate.

"I want nothing from you," it said, its tone softer now. "I've seen your journey, seen your struggle. But you cannot stop the shadow by fighting it directly. That is its power—to make you fear it, to break you from the inside out. You must understand it."

Enola's breath caught. The shadow was more than just a creature of the dark. It was something deeper, tied to the city's very soul, to the forgotten history beneath its cracked surface.

"How do we stop it?" Enola's voice trembled with the weight of the question, her mind racing with the possibilities. Was it possible to even stop something so ancient, so deeply embedded in the world's fabric?

The figure's eyes dimmed, as if they, too, carried the burden of that knowledge. "You must face the past. The heart of the city, where the shadow began, is the only place where it can be undone. But..."

The figure paused, and for the first time, there was a trace of uncertainty in its voice. "There is another way—a more dangerous way. But it requires a sacrifice. A choice."

Enola's pulse quickened. "A sacrifice? What do you mean? What choice?"

The figure took a step forward, its movements unnervingly smooth, as if it were one with the very air around it. "You must choose to let the past die. Or, if you choose wrong, the shadow will consume everything—everything you've fought for, everything you care about."

The room seemed to tighten around her, the shadow twitching and jerking as it tried to break free of its invisible binds. Enola's heart pounded in her chest. Was there truly a way to stop this nightmare? Could she really let go of everything that tied her to this place—her past, her memories, everything that made her who she was?

The figure's voice dropped to a whisper, barely audible against the deafening growl of the shadow, "The choice lies with you. And if you fail, it will be the end of all."

Enola stepped forward, her mind a whirlwind. The future seemed to stretch out before her—a thousand possibilities, none of them clear, none of them safe. Her claws dug into the ground, the pressure of the moment bearing down on her.

Then, in the instant before she could speak, the shadow broke free.

It surged forward, more powerful than ever, its tendrils whirling through the air with unrelenting speed.

Chapter 20

The air around Enola crackled with raw energy as the shadow surged forward, its form now fully unleashed. The figure in front of her seemed to vanish into the wind, swallowed by the very darkness it had been attempting to control. The tendrils of the shadow whipped through the air, closer, faster, their chilling presence almost suffocating.

Enola's heart pounded in her chest, but the weight of the figure's words—of the choice she now faced—remained heavy on her mind. She could feel Rook beside her, his body taut with readiness, his eyes locked onto the swirling darkness. They couldn't fight it head-on; she knew that now. The figure had been right. Fighting the shadow would only feed it, strengthen it.

But how could she stop it? How could she let the past die when she didn't even understand it fully?

"Enola, now!" Rook growled, his voice urgent, snapping her back to reality.

She barely had time to react. The shadow's tendrils lashed out, streaking toward her with a speed that left no room for hesitation. Enola's instincts screamed at her to run, but she held her ground.

The choice.

She thought back to the figure's words. "Let the past die. Or it consumes everything." Was there any way to do that without destroying herself in the process?

With a quick glance to Rook, Enola made a decision.

She reached down to her side, claws grazing the ground as she pushed off with all her strength, charging toward the heart of the shadow's fury. The wind howled around her, a high-pitched screeching that was almost human in its desperation. The shadow closed in, its tendrils reaching for her, coiling and twisting with dark energy.

But Enola didn't stop. She ran straight into it, bracing herself for the impact, hoping beyond hope that she had made the right choice.

Suddenly, everything went still.

The tendrils of the shadow seemed to freeze mid-air, suspended in some unseen force. Enola skidded to a halt just inches from the darkness. It was as if time itself had stopped—everything hung in the balance.

Then, the silence was shattered.

A voice, one that echoed through her very soul, broke through the quiet.

"You've made your choice."

Enola's heart skipped a beat. She turned around, searching for the source of the voice, but there was no one there. No figure, no sign of movement. Only the vast, oppressive blackness that seemed to stretch on forever.

The shadow swirled around her, thick and choking. But instead of consuming her, it seemed to be... waiting. Watching.

"What now?" she whispered to the air, her voice trembling, unsure if anyone would hear her.

The answer came not in words, but in a flash of light. A blinding, searing light that cut through the dark, illuminating the world around her in a stark, unnatural brilliance. The ground beneath her feet trembled, cracks forming in the concrete as if the city itself were protesting her decision.

The shadow howled in fury, its form pulsing with a terrible, primal rage. But it could not move. It could not escape.

Enola stepped forward, the power of her choice propelling her. Rook was at her side in an instant, his body pressed against hers, his fur bristling with tension. Together, they moved closer to the heart of the shadow, toward the place where it had all started—the heart of the city, as the figure had said.

But as they approached, something shifted. A sudden, icy chill swept through the air, and Enola felt the unmistakable sensation of being watched.

The city was alive—it's very foundation seemed to pulse with energy. Something was changing, something huge.

And then, a voice spoke from the shadows.

"You should not have come here."

Enola's heart skipped again, her blood turning cold. This voice—it was different from the shadow's growls, from the figure's whispers. It was deeper, more commanding. And it wasn't coming from the darkness around them. It was coming from inside her mind.

A figure stepped out from the shadows.

Tall, cloaked in darkness, but with an unmistakable aura of power. Its form was indistinct, but Enola could feel its presence—like the weight of a thousand storms about to break. The air thickened with an unnatural pressure, and she couldn't breathe properly.

This wasn't the same thing she'd fought before. This was something far worse. Something older.

"I warned you," the figure continued, its voice a slow, painful whisper that made Enola's spine chill. "Now you must face the consequences of your choices. You are not prepared for what you've just unleashed."

Enola's mind raced. Was this... the true source of the shadow? The thing that had been waiting all this time? The one who had hidden in the city's heart?

Rook growled low beside her, his muscles coiling, ready to strike, but Enola stopped him with a single, urgent glance.

"We have no choice now," she whispered. "We have to stop it."

The figure's laugh was low, almost pitying. "Stop it?" it echoed, stepping closer, its shadow stretching out impossibly long across the broken ground. "You think you can stop it? You don't even understand what you've done."

The figure raised its hands, and the city trembled once again. With a sickening sound, the ground cracked open beneath them, sending shockwaves through the air.

Enola's heart dropped into her stomach as the city seemed to break apart before her eyes. Towers crumbled, the earth split open, and the city, the very heart of it, began to fall apart.

Chapter 21

he city crumbled around them, its decay more violent than ever. Enola could feel the ground shaking beneath her paws, the sound of falling debris deafening. She and Rook barely managed to stay on their feet as cracks spread outward like a spider's web, tearing through the very heart of the city.

The figure's words hung in the air, a terrible weight pressing down on Enola's chest. *You've unleashed the truth.*

But what truth? What had she done?

As the earth buckled beneath them, the shadow pulsed with an intensity Enola had never felt before. The darkness that had once seemed like an entity to be fought now felt like an ancient force, alive with purpose, and it was rising.

Rook's low growl pulled her back to the present. "Enola!" he barked. "We need to get out of here. Now!"

But Enola couldn't tear her gaze from the crumbling city. She could feel it—something was waking, something deep within the earth. The city had been built over something far older than she could have ever imagined, and now it was stirring, angry and forgotten.

"Rook," she murmured, her voice barely audible over the chaos, "what if this—this destruction—isn't just the shadow?"

Rook's eyes flashed with realization, but before he could speak, the ground beneath their paws buckled once again. They were thrown off balance, tumbling through the air as the world around them broke apart. Enola's heart raced as she instinctively reached out for Rook, grabbing him by the scruff of his neck and pulling him close.

Together, they landed with a hard thud on solid ground, the earth around them shifting violently. As Enola rose to her paws, a terrible crack split the air. From the centre of the city, a beam of light shot upward into the sky, as though the heavens themselves were being torn open. And within that light, something—someone—was emerging.

A figure, cloaked in an aura of pure energy, descended from the blinding beam. Its form was indistinct at first, like a shadow being carved from the light. But then, slowly, it began to solidify.

Enola's breath caught in her throat. This was no ordinary creature.

This was something ancient, something that had been dormant for centuries—perhaps longer. As the figure continued to materialize, Enola saw it clearly for the first time. It was a creature unlike any she had ever seen before, its eyes glowing with a cold, otherworldly light.

"Who... are you?" Enola asked, her voice trembling.

The figure's lips curled into a slow, knowing smile, and its voice echoed through the air like a distant thunderclap.

"You've awakened me," it said, its voice calm but laced with an overwhelming sense of power. "And for that, I thank you."

Enola's fur bristled. "What do you want?"

The creature's eyes narrowed. "What I want... is nothing. But what I need..." It paused, as if considering its next words carefully. "What I need is for you to understand. You were never meant to stop the shadow. You were never meant to stop me."

A shiver ran down Enola's spine as the realization hit her. The shadow—the destruction—they were all part of something much bigger. Something that had been planned, orchestrated, for eons. And she had unwittingly set it all into motion.

Rook stepped forward, his body tense. "If you think we're just going to let you destroy everything, you're wrong."

The creature tilted its head, its glowing eyes studying Rook with an unsettling calmness. "Oh, I'm not going to destroy everything. I'm going to rebuild it. From the ground up. A world of my own design."

Enola's blood ran cold. "What do you mean, rebuild?"

The figure smiled again, and this time, there was no warmth in it. "You'll see soon enough. You've only just begun to grasp the extent of the power you've awakened. The shadow is my tool, my servant. And now, it is stronger than ever. But it will not be enough. I will need more. More like you."

"Like us?" Enola repeated, her mind reeling. "What do you mean, like us?"

But before the creature could answer, the sky above them suddenly darkened, as if the sun had been swallowed whole. The light from the beam flickered, sputtering in the air before going out entirely, leaving them in complete and utter darkness.

A pulse of energy surged through the ground, so strong that it nearly knocked them off their feet. The air grew thick, heavy with a strange and suffocating pressure. Enola looked around, trying to make sense of what was happening, but everything was shifting, changing in ways that defied reason.

And then, from the darkness, came the whispers.

Soft at first, like the faintest rustling of leaves, but growing louder with every passing moment. They were coming from all directions, surrounding them, pressing in. The shadows themselves seemed to be speaking, their voices a strange, melodic hum that cut through the silence like a knife.

Enola's pulse quickened. *What are they saying?*

She couldn't understand the words, but the fear they instilled was palpable. Whatever this was, it was unlike anything she had ever faced.

"We need to get out of here," Rook growled, his body tense with apprehension. "Now."

Enola nodded, her mind racing. But before they could move, the whispers reached a crescendo, and the ground beneath them cracked open, splitting wide with an earth-shattering roar. A massive shadow rose from the depths of the fissure, its form twisted and writhing. It was no longer a creature of simple darkness—it was something far worse. Something alive.

And as the ground trembled beneath their paws, the shadow began to rise.

"RUN!"

Chapter 22

The city crumbled around them, its decay more violent than ever. Enola could feel the ground shaking beneath her paws, the sound of falling debris deafening. She and Rook barely managed to stay on their feet as cracks spread outward like a spider's web, tearing through the very heart of the city.

The figure's words hung in the air, a terrible weight pressing down on Enola's chest. *You've unleashed the truth.*

But what truth? What had she done?

As the earth buckled beneath them, the shadow pulsed with an intensity Enola had never felt before. The darkness that had once seemed like an entity to be fought now felt like an ancient force, alive with purpose, and it was rising.

Rook's low growl pulled her back to the present. "Enola!" he barked. "We need to get out of here. Now!"

But Enola couldn't tear her gaze from the crumbling city. She could feel it—something was waking, something deep within the earth. The city had been built over something far older than she could have ever imagined, and now it was stirring, angry and forgotten.

"Rook," she murmured, her voice barely audible over the chaos, "what if this—this destruction—isn't just the shadow?"

Rook's eyes flashed with realization, but before he could speak, the ground beneath their paws buckled once again. They were thrown off balance, tumbling through the air as the world around them broke apart. Enola's heart raced as she instinctively reached out for Rook, grabbing him by the scruff of his neck and pulling him close.

Together, they landed with a hard thud on solid ground, the earth around them shifting violently. As Enola rose to her paws, a terrible crack split the air. From the centre of the city, a beam of light shot upward into the sky, as though the heavens themselves were being torn open. And within that light, something—someone—was emerging.

A figure, cloaked in an aura of pure energy, descended from the blinding beam. Its form was indistinct at first, like a shadow being carved from the light. But then, slowly, it began to solidify.

Enola's breath caught in her throat. This was no ordinary creature.

This was something ancient, something that had been dormant for centuries—perhaps longer. As the figure continued to materialize, Enola saw it clearly for the first time. It was a creature unlike any she had ever seen before, its eyes glowing with a cold, otherworldly light.

"Who... are you?" Enola asked, her voice trembling.

The figure's lips curled into a slow, knowing smile, and its voice echoed through the air like a distant thunderclap.

"You've awakened me," it said, its voice calm but laced with an overwhelming sense of power. "And for that, I thank you."

Enola's fur bristled. "What do you want?"

The creature's eyes narrowed. "What I want... is nothing. But what I need..." It paused, as if considering its next words carefully. "What I need is for you to understand. You were never meant to stop the shadow. You were never meant to stop me."

A shiver ran down Enola's spine as the realization hit her. The shadow—the destruction—they were all part of something much bigger. Something that had been planned, orchestrated, for eons. And she had unwittingly set it all into motion.

Rook stepped forward, his body tense. "If you think we're just going to let you destroy everything, you're wrong."

The creature tilted its head, its glowing eyes studying Rook with an unsettling calmness. "Oh, I'm not going to destroy everything. I'm going to rebuild it. From the ground up. A world of my own design."

Enola's blood ran cold. "What do you mean, rebuild?"

The figure smiled again, and this time, there was no warmth in it. "You'll see soon enough. You've only just begun to grasp the extent of the power you've awakened. The shadow is my tool, my servant. And now, it is stronger than ever. But it will not be enough. I will need more. More like you."

"Like us?" Enola repeated, her mind reeling. "What do you mean, like us?"

But before the creature could answer, the sky above them suddenly darkened, as if the sun had been swallowed whole. The light from the beam flickered, sputtering in the air before going out entirely, leaving them in complete and utter darkness.

A pulse of energy surged through the ground, so strong that it nearly knocked them off their feet. The air grew thick, heavy with a strange and suffocating pressure. Enola looked around, trying to make sense of what was happening, but everything was shifting, changing in ways that defied reason.

And then, from the darkness, came the whispers.

Soft at first, like the faintest rustling of leaves, but growing louder with every passing moment. They were coming from all directions, surrounding them, pressing in. The shadows themselves seemed to be speaking, their voices a strange, melodic hum that cut through the silence like a knife.

Enola's pulse quickened. *What are they saying?*

She couldn't understand the words, but the fear they instilled was palpable. Whatever this was, it was unlike anything she had ever faced.

"We need to get out of here," Rook growled, his body tense with apprehension. "Now."

Enola nodded, her mind racing. But before they could move, the whispers reached a crescendo, and the ground beneath them cracked open, splitting wide with an earth-shattering roar. A massive shadow rose from the depths of the fissure, its form twisted and writhing. It was no longer a creature of simple darkness—it was something far worse. Something alive.

And as the ground trembled beneath their paws, the shadow began to rise.

"RUN!"

Chapter 23

The air around them thickened with a coldness that sliced through Enola's fur. Her heart pounded in her chest as she and Rook stumbled back, their paws scrambling for traction on the shifting ground. The shadow, a formless mass of writhing darkness, continued to rise from the depths of the city. It loomed over them, a towering presence, its shape impossible to define, as though the very darkness had come alive.

"Rook!" Enola shouted, her voice drowned out by the growls and deep hums reverberating through the earth. "We need to move! Now!"

Rook didn't need any further encouragement. With a swift glance to Enola, he lunged forward, his muscles coiled with panic and determination. Enola followed close behind, her mind racing. They had no time to think—only time to run. The shadow seemed to stretch across the entire city, its tendrils reaching toward them, grasping at the air like the hands of some ancient, forgotten god.

With every step they took, the ground beneath them seemed to quake harder, the tremors making it difficult to stay upright. The shadow's form twisted, pulsating with an eerie glow that lit up the darkened streets. It was as if the shadow was a living thing, feeding off the fear that radiated from them, growing stronger with every passing second.

Enola's paws hit the cracked pavement in a blur, but it wasn't fast enough. Behind them, the shadow surged forward with an unnatural speed, its tendrils like serpents racing to close the distance. She could hear it—the distant whispers growing louder, more insistent, as if the shadow itself was speaking directly into her mind.

You cannot escape me.

The voice echoed inside her head, deep and full of malice. Enola gritted her teeth, forcing herself to focus on the path ahead. There was no room for hesitation, no room for fear. If they didn't find shelter, if they didn't get far enough, they wouldn't survive.

Rook barked over his shoulder, his voice sharp with urgency. "Head for the tunnels! They might be our only chance!"

Enola didn't hesitate. She knew what tunnels he meant—the old, forgotten underpasses that wound beneath the city like a maze. It was their only hope. She pushed herself harder, her legs burning, her chest tight with the effort.

The shadow's tendrils snapped out, just missing Rook by a whisker as they darted down an alley, desperate to find the entrance. Enola felt the air shift, the temperature plummeting even further as the shadow grew closer. She dared not look behind her; she could feel its presence closing in, its whispers growing louder, more insistent.

You cannot hide from me.

They rounded a corner, and Enola spotted the rusted metal grate of the tunnel entrance half-buried in debris. With a burst of adrenaline, she charged forward and shoved it open, Rook hot on her heels. The tunnel's cold, stale air hit her face like a slap, but it was a welcome reprieve from the suffocating grip of the shadow.

They scrambled down the narrow passageway, the walls too close for comfort, the echoes of their breathing deafening in the silence. The whispers from above seemed to follow them, reverberating in the dark, but the shadow itself was no longer immediately above them. Enola's paws flew over the damp stone, and she could feel the faint tremors of the ground above them, a reminder that the city was dying, and it was dying fast.

Rook slowed, panting heavily. His gaze met Enola's with a grim understanding. "This won't last. The tunnels won't protect us forever."

Enola nodded, her heart hammering in her chest. She knew Rook was right. They were safe for now, but not for long. The shadow would find them. It always found its prey.

"We need answers," Enola said, her voice hoarse from the running. "The dogs—what they said about the heart of the city—there has to be something there. Something we can use."

Rook's eyes darkened, and he looked down the tunnel, his ears flicking back. "If the heart of the city is where this thing began, then we're heading straight into its lair. We don't know what we'll find there."

"I know," Enola said quietly. "But we don't have a choice. We can't outrun this thing forever."

There was a long pause before Rook nodded, his face set in determination. "Then we find a way to end it. Once and for all."

They continued down the tunnel in silence, the weight of their decision hanging heavy in the air. But every step they took, the closer they came to the heart of the city—and to the shadow's source.

The tunnel twisted and turned, winding deeper into the earth as if pulling them further away from the surface world. The faint hum of the city above them grew quieter, replaced by the eerie stillness of the underground. It felt as though the very air was holding its breath.

Eventually, they reached a large chamber, its walls damp and slick with age. The faint light from their eyes reflected off the stone, casting long, distorted shadows. There was no clear exit—just more tunnels leading into the unknown.

Enola's gaze flicked nervously to the entrance. The sounds of the shadow's whispers were muffled now, but that didn't mean it was gone. No, it was still out there, waiting for its moment to strike.

Rook stopped at the centre of the chamber, his body tense. "What now?"

Enola scanned the walls, her mind racing. The dogs had said that the heart of the city held the key to stopping the shadow, but they hadn't said what exactly they'd find there. And there was no telling how much time they had before the shadow found its way underground.

Then, in the far corner of the chamber, Enola saw it—a faint glow coming from a small crack in the wall. It was barely noticeable, but it pulsed with a strange energy, like the heartbeat of the city itself.

Without speaking, Enola moved toward it, her paws quiet against the stone floor. Rook followed closely behind, his eyes wary.

When they reached the crack, Enola knelt down, pressing her paw against the wall. The glow intensified, and as if responding to her touch, the wall shifted, revealing a narrow passage leading deeper into the darkness.

A sense of foreboding washed over her. She wasn't sure what lay ahead, but she knew they had no choice but to follow the path. There was only one way out of this—and it was through whatever lay beyond this secret passage.

"Ready?" Enola whispered to Rook.

He nodded, his voice low and steady. "As ready as I'll ever be."

They stepped forward into the darkness, the shadows closing in around them. As they entered the passage, the faint glow from the crack suddenly dimmed, and the tunnel seemed to collapse in on itself. The walls shook violently, and the very ground beneath them cracked open once more.

From the depths of the passage, a new sound emerged—low, rumbling, and familiar. The shadow was moving faster now.

And it was coming for them.

Chapter 24

The tunnel seemed to stretch endlessly ahead, its walls closing in as if the very city itself were shifting, distorting, preparing to swallow them whole. The faint glow from the crack in the wall had almost completely faded, leaving them in a darkness so complete it pressed against their bodies. Every breath Enola took seemed to echo, amplifying the silence that threatened to swallow her thoughts.

Rook's paw steps were close behind her, his presence a steady anchor in the growing chaos. Still, even with him beside her, the feeling of something watching them, something ancient and relentless, crawled under her skin. The shadow was no longer just a whisper—it was a presence. A force. It was hunting them, and it was getting closer.

"Stay sharp," Rook muttered, his voice barely a whisper in the suffocating dark. "This place feels... wrong."

Enola didn't respond immediately. She was too focused on the growing hum that vibrated through the ground. It wasn't a sound—it was a pulse. A steady, rhythmic pulse that matched the beat of her own heart. The further they went, the more intense it became.

Ahead, the tunnel seemed to open into something far larger, the walls falling away to reveal a vast chamber. Enola could feel the air change—thicker now, heavy with the scent of decay and old memories. This was it. The heart of the city. The place where it all began.

She stopped at the entrance, her breath shallow as she took in the sight before her. The chamber was vast—more like an underground temple than anything else. The floor was made of smooth stone, worn by the passage of time, and strange, runic symbols covered the walls, glowing faintly in the dim light.

At the centre of the room was a massive, circular platform, cracked and broken by years of neglect. But what truly drew Enola's attention was what lay at its centre.

A stone altar, covered in layers of dust and old, crumbling offerings. It was both ancient and familiar, as though it had always been there, waiting for them. But the most disturbing part was what stood atop the altar.

A crystal. A dark, jagged crystal, pulsing with the same energy that had haunted them since they first encountered the shadow. It was enormous—larger than anything Enola had ever seen—and it seemed to hum with life, its edges crackling with dark energy.

Rook stepped forward cautiously, his eyes scanning the room. "This is it, isn't it?" His voice was heavy with disbelief.

Enola didn't answer right away. Instead, she took a few tentative steps toward the altar, the hum of the crystal growing louder with every movement she made. She could feel its energy coursing through the air, a weight pressing down on her chest, suffocating her.

"Whatever this is," Enola whispered, her voice trembling, "it's the source. This is where the shadow began."

The floor trembled beneath their paws as the hum from the crystal intensified, growing louder until it seemed to shake the very walls of the chamber. Enola's fur stood on end, a deep, instinctual fear clenching her gut. She couldn't help but feel like something was waking, something ancient and powerful that had been dormant for far too long.

And then, a voice—cold, impossibly deep—echoed through the chamber, a low rumble that vibrated in her bones.

You should not have come here.

Enola froze. The voice was everywhere, inside her head, in the air around her, in the very walls of the chamber. It felt like the city itself was speaking. The shadow had found them—and it was speaking through the crystal.

"Rook!" Enola shouted, her heart racing. "We need to leave—now!"

But as she turned to flee, the ground beneath their paws shifted again, the stone cracking and splitting. A low growl filled the air as a dark shape began to materialize in the centre of the room. At first, it was just a shadow—a silhouette—but it quickly took form, its outline becoming clearer with every passing second.

The shape that emerged was taller than any creature Enola had ever seen. It was humanoid in form but twisted, its body made of the same dark energy as the shadow itself. Its eyes were empty voids, blacker than the deepest night, and they locked onto Enola and Rook with a chilling intensity.

"You are too late," the creature growled, its voice like the sound of shifting stone. "The city's heart has awakened, and with it, so have I. The shadow is no longer just a force—it is my will, my power. And it will consume everything."

The air thickened with malice as the creature's form shifted, its limbs stretching and twisting in unnatural ways. It was growing stronger by the second, feeding off the energy of the crystal, the heart of the city itself.

Enola's paws scraped against the stone floor, her body moving on instinct as she backed toward Rook. She could feel the oppressive weight of the creature's presence bearing down on her, its power suffocating. But she couldn't stop now. They had to stop it, or all was lost.

"What... what is it?" Rook muttered, his voice full of awe and fear. He was shaking, though he was trying to hide it behind a mask of defiance.

Enola's mind raced, trying to make sense of what she was seeing. She had heard rumours, ancient stories told in hushed whispers among the cats—legends of the city's fall, of a dark entity that had once ruled the land, its power sealed away beneath the city. This creature... it had to be the one from the stories.

"It's the one who caused the city's downfall," Enola said, barely above a whisper. "It's the reason the shadow exists. And it's waking up."

Rook's eyes widened, and for the first time, Enola saw true fear in his gaze. "Then we're too late."

The creature's form continued to shift, its body becoming more solid, more real. It was no longer just a shadow—it was a force of nature, a being of pure malevolence. And it was ready to reclaim the city.

"I will bring about the end," the creature hissed, its voice a chorus of whispers. "The shadow is my army. And it will devour everything in its path."

Enola's heart hammered in her chest. She knew what she had to do. They couldn't let this creature complete its resurrection. They had to stop it now.

But as she moved toward the crystal, the ground beneath her paws cracked wide open, and the room began to shake violently. The walls collapsed inward, the ceiling cracking above them. There was no more time.

With one last desperate glance at Rook, Enola lunged forward, her claws reaching for the crystal, hoping against hope that she could destroy it before it was too late.

Just as her claws touched the crystal, the ground beneath her feet shattered entirely, and the world seemed to tear apart around them. The last thing she saw before the darkness swallowed her whole was the creature's glowing eyes—and the sound of the city crumbling, a death knell for everything they had fought to protect.

Chapter 25

The ground cracked beneath their paws, the world around them collapsing into chaos as the creature's deep voice rumbled in the air. Enola's heart raced, the weight of the moment pressing down on her. The crystal—its power was the key, the heart of the shadow, and the only way to stop the creature from fully awakening.

But as her claws reached out to touch the dark crystal, the earth beneath her feet shuddered violently, sending shockwaves through the chamber. She barely had time to register the danger before the floor beneath them shattered entirely.

"No!" Rook's voice echoed in the chaos, but it was too late.

The ground split open, the chamber tumbling into nothingness. Enola felt herself falling, the air rushing past her as the darkness swallowed them whole. She could hear Rook's frantic shouts, but they were drowned by the deafening roar of the city crumbling around them. The shadow had won.

And then, silence.

Enola opened her eyes, her body aching, her mind disoriented. She was no longer in the chamber—the city, the crystal, the creature... everything was gone. But there was no peace. No respite.

Rook was beside her, still alive but shaken. The cold air burned her lungs as she pushed herself up, her limbs trembling beneath her.

"Where are we?" she whispered, looking around.

The space around them was strange—surreal. They were standing on the edge of a vast, empty expanse. The air was thick with the same darkness that had consumed the city, and in the distance, Enola could just make out the shape of the creature, looming in the distance, its glowing eyes like twin beacons in the void.

"It's... not over," Enola said, the realization hitting her with full force. "The creature—it's still alive."

Rook looked toward her, his expression grim. "Then we'll have to finish this, no matter where it takes us."

But the world was no longer familiar. The city, the tunnel, the altar—all of it had been shattered, scattered across a vast, unknown landscape. They were in the heart of the shadow now, where no light could penetrate, where the rules of the world no longer applied.

The creature's voice came again, but this time, it was not from behind them.

You cannot escape, Enola. You have already lost.

The voice seemed to come from everywhere, its power vibrating through the very air, the ground, the soul itself. The shadow wasn't just a force anymore—it was a presence that had consumed the very fabric of their reality.

Rook's claws dug into the ground, his face a mask of determination. "We're not done. Not yet."

Enola nodded, despite the fear that gripped her. She didn't know how they would stop the creature, but she knew they had no other choice.

The creature's form began to take shape again, darker, more solid, as it closed in on them. It was no longer just a shadow—it was a being of pure malice, its glowing eyes the only thing that seemed to cut through the endless dark.

Enola's pulse quickened as she prepared for what was to come. She didn't know how they would survive this—but she would fight until the very end.

And as the creature's voice reached them once more, Enola understood: The battle had only just begun.

Chapter 26

The ground cracked beneath their paws, the world around them collapsing into chaos as the creature's deep voice rumbled in the air. Enola's heart raced, the weight of the moment pressing down on her. The crystal—its power was the key, the heart of the shadow, and the only way to stop the creature from fully awakening.

But as her claws reached out to touch the dark crystal, the earth beneath her feet shuddered violently, sending shockwaves through the chamber. She barely had time to register the danger before the floor beneath them shattered entirely.

"No!" Rook's voice echoed in the chaos, but it was too late.

The ground split open, the chamber tumbling into nothingness. Enola felt herself falling, the air rushing past her as the darkness swallowed them whole. She could hear Rook's frantic shouts, but they were drowned by the deafening roar of the city crumbling around them. The shadow had won.

And then, silence.

Enola opened her eyes, her body aching, her mind disoriented. She was no longer in the chamber—the city, the crystal, the creature... everything was gone. But there was no peace. No respite.

Rook was beside her, still alive but shaken. The cold air burned her lungs as she pushed herself up, her limbs trembling beneath her.

"Where are we?" she whispered, looking around.

The space around them was strange—surreal. They were standing on the edge of a vast, empty expanse. The air was thick with the same darkness that had consumed the city, and in the distance, Enola could just make out the shape of the creature, looming in the distance, its glowing eyes like twin beacons in the void.

"It's... not over," Enola said, the realization hitting her with full force. "The creature—it's still alive."

Rook looked toward her, his expression grim. "Then we'll have to finish this, no matter where it takes us."

But the world was no longer familiar. The city, the tunnel, the altar—all of it had been shattered, scattered across a vast, unknown landscape. They were in the heart of the shadow now, where no light could penetrate, where the rules of the world no longer applied.

The creature's voice came again, but this time, it was not from behind them.

You cannot escape, Enola. You have already lost.

The voice seemed to come from everywhere, its power vibrating through the very air, the ground, the soul itself. The shadow wasn't just a force anymore—it was a presence that had consumed the very fabric of their reality.

Rook's claws dug into the ground, his face a mask of determination. "We're not done. Not yet."

Enola nodded, despite the fear that gripped her. She didn't know how they would stop the creature, but she knew they had no other choice.

The creature's form began to take shape again, darker, more solid, as it closed in on them. It was no longer just a shadow—it was a being of pure malice, its glowing eyes the only thing that seemed to cut through the endless dark.

But as the creature's form solidified further, Enola's heart skipped a beat. The silhouette before them was unmistakable, its shape too familiar.

The creature's form began to shift, changing again, as though the darkness around it was peeling away. Enola's breath caught in her throat.

And then, the shadows cleared completely.

Standing before them, not as the towering, monstrous form they had fought, but as a figure both familiar and terrifying, was someone Enola had never expected. The creature—was not a being of pure shadow, but a cat. A cat she had known her entire life.

Enola's mouth went dry as the creature's glowing eyes locked with hers. It was Korr.

"Korr?" she whispered, the word barely leaving her lips as she stumbled back, her mind struggling to make sense of what she was seeing. The friend she thought had been lost to the darkness, the brave and loyal cat who had fought by her side, was now standing in front of her—changed. Corrupted.

The creature—or Korr, now—smiled cruelly, a twisted grin that sent chills down Enola's spine.

"You were always so certain, Enola," Korr said, his voice now deep and echoing, as though layered with the power of the shadow itself. "You never questioned the source of the shadow. The darkness. You thought it was just a force, a simple thing to defeat. But it was never just that. It was me. It was always me."

Rook stepped forward, his claws bared, his voice shaking with disbelief. "Korr? What... what are you saying? You're the one who was trying to save the city!"

"I was," Korr replied, his tone colder now, eyes filled with a twisted sense of amusement. "I was trying to save it. From *you*. From all of you. You think you understand the shadow, but you never asked the right questions. You never saw the truth."

Enola could barely breathe, the weight of his words pressing on her like a physical force. She had known Korr. Trusted him. Fought beside him. And now—now he was the very thing they had been fighting all along.

"You were always too blinded by hope to see it," Korr continued. "The shadow didn't consume me, Enola. I *embraced* it. I became it. I became everything that was forgotten, everything that was left behind. And now, I'm the future of this world."

The revelation hit Enola like a blow to the chest. The monster they had fought was never a mere force—it had been Korr all along. The friend who had once fought beside them had been consumed by his own darkness, transformed into the very thing he had once feared.

"We can't let this happen," Rook said, his voice filled with rage. "We won't let you destroy everything we've worked for!"

Korr's eyes glowed brighter, his shadowy form growing even larger as he stepped forward, his dark presence overwhelming the space around them.

"You don't understand, Rook," Korr said, his voice no longer familiar, but the guttural growl of a creature long past redemption. "This is not about destruction. This is about evolution. This world was doomed to fall. But I—*I*—will rebuild it. In my image. In the image of the shadow."

Enola's pulse raced. There was no turning back now. The battle they thought they had won had been a lie. Korr wasn't just part of the shadow's power—he had become the heart of it.

She looked to Rook, his eyes filled with a shared understanding. They had to stop him. There was no choice now.

But as the creature—Korr—advanced, the ground beneath them trembled again. The battle was far from over.

Chapter 27

The landscape around them had shifted again. The darkness was now an oppressive force that seemed to bend reality itself, warping the air and the earth. Every step they took seemed to echo in a hollow silence, each footfall heavier than the last.

Enola and Rook moved side by side, their eyes focused on the faint glow in the distance—the crystal. It pulsed rhythmically, casting an eerie light that danced across the jagged rocks of this new, nightmarish realm. The creature, Korr—his monstrous form—hovered nearby, watching them from the shadows.

Rook's fur was bristled with tension, his claws digging into the ground as if to ground himself, to remind himself that he was still there, still fighting.

"We can do this," Enola murmured, her voice barely above a whisper, though her heart was racing.

"We have to," Rook replied, his gaze steady despite the deep fear that gnawed at him.

But as they drew closer to the crystal, the ground beneath them began to tremble. It was as if the earth itself was alive, shifting beneath their paws to stop them from advancing.

A deep, resonant hum filled the air—a sound that made their bones vibrate. The crystal was alive, pulsing with the dark energy of the shadow. Enola could feel the oppressive weight of its power, pressing down on them with every step they took.

"We need to destroy it," Enola said, her voice trembling despite her resolve. "It's the only way to stop Korr, to stop all of this."

Rook nodded, but before either of them could take another step, a sudden surge of energy erupted from the crystal. It wasn't just the dark power of the shadow—it was something else, something ancient and primal. The air crackled with an electric charge, sharp and biting. Enola felt it first, a strange pulse of power that surged through her body. But it wasn't her pain—it was Rook's.

"Rook!" she shouted, turning to see him stagger back, his body arching in agony. His paws scraped the ground as his fur stood on end. "What's happening?!"

Rook gasped, his eyes wide with shock. "It's... it's hurting me. The power—it's like... like it knows me."

Enola felt the weight of the words settle over her. This wasn't just the crystal's energy—it was targeting Rook directly. His connection to the crystal, to the shadow, seemed deeper than she realized.

The truth hit her like a blow to the chest. The creature hadn't just possessed Korr—it had possessed Rook too, long before they even realized it. The creature had been manipulating him, drawing on his fears and desires to feed the shadow's power. And now, that bond was manifesting, in full force.

"Rook!" Enola cried out, rushing to his side. "You've got to fight it! You have to break free!"

But Rook couldn't speak. His body was rigid, trembling under the weight of the dark energy flowing through him. It was as if the crystal's power had become a direct conduit into his very soul. Enola could see the shadow rising inside him, its tendrils wrapping around his mind, suffocating him.

"No!" Enola screamed, desperately trying to pull him away from the crystal's influence. "This isn't you, Rook! You can fight it!"

The hum of the crystal grew louder, its rhythm quicker, more insistent. Enola could feel it, too—it's cold, suffocating presence closing in on her. It was as if the crystal was testing them, toying with their resolve. And it had chosen Rook as its first victim.

Suddenly, a deep voice boomed from the darkness, reverberating in their minds like a nightmare made real.

"You cannot destroy me," the creature—Korr—spoke, his form still hidden in the shadows. "You cannot fight what is already within you."

Enola looked around frantically, desperate for a way to break through the crystal's hold over Rook. She couldn't do this alone. She needed him.

"Rook!" she pleaded. "Please, listen to me! We're fighting this together. You've always been there for me. Now, I need you."

For a heartbeat, there was nothing—no response. But then, Enola saw it: a flicker in Rook's eyes, a glimmer of the old strength that had always defined him. He was still there. The shadow hadn't completely consumed him yet.

With all her strength, Enola pushed against the pressure that was bearing down on them both. She was still holding Rook, her paws pressing against his trembling form, her mind reaching out to him, trying to connect with the part of him that was still Rook.

"Fight it!" she screamed, the words burning through her chest. "You are not just a weapon! You're not just a part of the shadow! You're stronger than this!"

And then, slowly, Rook's body began to relax, the tension in his muscles easing. His breath came in ragged gasps, and the energy that had been writhing inside him began to dissipate.

"I... I'm... not..." he muttered, his voice strained but filled with clarity. "I'm not the shadow."

Enola held him tighter, her heart soaring with relief. "You're not. You're you, Rook."

But the battle wasn't over. With Rook still fighting the dark power inside him, Enola turned back to the crystal. The creature's voice echoed louder now, mocking them, warning them.

"You cannot stop me," Korr's voice hissed, louder and more ferocious. "I am everything that has been consumed. You cannot escape your fate."

Enola's gaze locked on the crystal, the pulsing light casting shadows across her face. The creature, Korr—he was right. They were fighting against a force that had always existed, one that was deeply rooted in the very essence of the world.

But Enola knew what she had to do. It was now or never.

With all her strength, she lunged at the crystal once more, her claws sinking into its jagged surface. The air around them crackled violently as the shadow's presence fought to keep her away. She could feel the crystal fighting back, sending shocks of pain through her body, but she didn't stop.

As Rook stood beside her, his breath laboured but steady, Enola gave one final, desperate pull.

The crystal shattered with a deafening crack.

And for the first time, the shadow's power began to wane. The weight of it lifted from their shoulders, the oppressive darkness fading. The hum that had vibrated through the ground ceased, and the pressure in the air slowly subsided.

Korr's voice let out a final, anguished scream, and the last remnants of his form dissolved into nothingness.

For a brief moment, there was nothing but silence.

Chapter 28

The crystal's destruction had sent a shockwave through the landscape, but the silence that followed felt even more deafening. Enola stood in the aftermath, her paws coated in dust and the shattered remnants of the crystal. The air was still thick with the remnants of dark energy, but it was no longer oppressive. The shadow had lifted, but it left a bitter, hollow feeling in its wake.

Rook stood beside her, his body still trembling, his fur matted with the last traces of the shadow's grip. His eyes, once full of fire and determination, were now clouded with exhaustion and pain. Enola's heart ached as she looked at him. She could still feel the pull of the creature's power inside him, faint but persistent, like a ghost haunting his mind.

"We did it," Enola said, her voice hoarse. The words felt hollow even as she spoke them. The battle was over, but she knew they hadn't won yet—not truly.

Rook didn't respond at first. His body seemed to be recovering, but his gaze was distant, as though he was still lost somewhere within the darkness that had nearly consumed him.

Enola stepped closer to him, her heart heavy. "Rook," she whispered, her voice gentle, "you're safe. We won. The creature—Korr—it's gone."

Rook's ears twitched, and he finally turned to face her. There was something in his eyes—something she hadn't seen before, something that spoke of the battle he had fought within himself. "It's not over, Enola," he said quietly. "There's still so much I don't understand... about what happened, about the shadow inside me."

She could see the weight of his words, the burden he carried. Enola's own heart felt torn. She wanted to say everything would be okay, but she knew the road ahead would be harder than they could imagine.

"We'll figure it out," she said firmly, her paw reaching out to rest on his shoulder. "Together."

Rook gave a weak smile, but it didn't reach his eyes. "Yeah. Together."

The wind stirred the dust around them as the landscape began to settle, the remnants of the city barely visible in the distance. Enola's mind raced, thinking of the others—the gang. They needed to know what had happened. They needed to regroup, to figure out what came next.

"I need to gather the others," she said, pulling away from Rook with a final glance. "We'll need everyone's help. There's still more to do."

Rook nodded, his expression softening. "Go. I'll be okay for now."

Enola turned away and began to make her way through the desolate landscape, her mind focused on one goal: finding the others.

The air was still thick with the echoes of the battle, but the world seemed quieter now. The endless expanse of empty land stretched before her, a constant reminder of the destruction the creature had wrought. She had to find the gang—Korr's influence was gone, but the void it had left needed to be filled with hope, with action. There was still work to do, and it was up to them to rebuild.

It didn't take long for Enola to find them. She knew where they would be—by the old remnants of the city, near the broken streets where they had once fought side by side. They were there, waiting, standing in silence as though they had felt the end of the battle before it had even come.

Korr's former allies—those who had fought against the creature, the gang—stood together, their faces worn with the weight of the fight they had just endured. They looked at Enola as she approached, their expressions a mix of uncertainty and relief.

"Enola," Korr's old friend, Korr's ally, called to her first, his voice quiet but filled with understanding. "It's over, isn't it?"

Enola nodded, her eyes scanning the faces of the others. "Yes, it's over. But it's not finished yet. The shadow is gone, but we need to heal. We need to rebuild what was lost."

The group shifted uneasily, their gazes flicking to Rook, who stood slightly behind her, his body still recovering, though he had a strong air of determination about him.

"I know we've all lost something," Enola continued, her voice steady. "We've all been touched by the darkness, some more than others. But we have to come together, now more than ever. We have to rebuild this world—our world."

There was a long silence before one of the cats, a burly tabby named Theo, stepped forward. "And what about him?" he asked, his eyes flicking to Rook. "We saw what happened. We all saw how he fought against the shadow. But... is he really safe?"

Rook flinched at the question, and Enola stepped forward, putting herself between him and the others. "He's not the creature. He's not Korr. He's Rook. And he's not alone in this."

Theo's gaze softened, but there was still doubt in his eyes. "We don't know what we're dealing with here. That shadow—it wasn't just a force. It had control over us."

Enola's heart sank as she realized the weight of what they were saying. The creature's hold had been over them all. Korr's presence, the darkness, it had lingered far longer than they had imagined. But now, the gang needed to decide if they would accept Rook, and if they could trust him again.

"We have to believe," Enola said softly, turning back to the group. "We have to believe in each other. We've all been through this, and we all deserve a chance to fight for what's left."

One by one, the group nodded. Slowly, uncertainty was replaced by resolve. They had fought together before, and now, they would fight to rebuild what had been lost.

"I'm with you," Korr's old ally said, stepping forward and offering a paw to Rook. "We all are."

Enola watched as the gang came together, the bonds forged through the battles and losses solidifying into something stronger. There was still a long road ahead of them, and the scars of the shadow's presence would never fully fade. But together, they would rebuild. Together, they would face whatever the future held.

And for the first time in what felt like forever, Enola felt hope. Not the fleeting hope that had once guided them, but a stronger, deeper hope—one built on the strength of their unity and the belief that they could overcome anything.

They weren't just fighting for survival anymore. They were fighting for a future.

Chapter 29

The first light of dawn stretched across the broken city, casting long shadows over the rubble. The air felt different—fresher, as though something in the world had shifted overnight. Enola could feel it deep within her, a quiet stirring that seemed to tell her the battle was over, but the war for the future was just beginning.

The sun had barely begun to rise when Enola gathered the remaining members of the gang. They were scattered across the camp, each in their own moment of reflection, still processing the enormity of what they had just been through. The shadow had been defeated, yes, but the weight of their survival lingered.

Enola stood tall, her fur matted and worn, but her gazing eyes clear, filled with the resolve that had gotten her this far. She had led them through the darkness, and now it was time to lead them into the light.

"We need to rebuild," she said, her voice steady, cutting through quiet murmurs of the gang. "What we've been through... it's more than anyone should have to endure. But we're still here. That means something."

Rook stepped forward, his movements slow but deliberate, the stiffness of his injuries evident. "Enola's right. The shadow's gone, but this city—it's still our home. If we give up now, everything we fought for means nothing."

A few of the gang members nodded. Korr stood silently, his usual boldness replaced by a contemplative stillness. He looked out at the ruins of the city and finally spoke. "We've seen what the darkness can do, how it can take everything from us. But we've also seen what happens when we stand together. Rebuilding won't be easy, but it's the only way forward."

Enola's gaze swept over the group. Some looked weary, others uncertain, but all of them were alive. They had faced the unthinkable and survived. That resilience, that strength, was what they needed now.

"We start small," she said. "We clear the streets, find shelter, and search for others who might still be out there. This city is more than just walls—it's the people in it."

Rook shifted on his paws, wincing slightly but nodding. "And when we find others, we'll remind them of what we've done. We'll show them it's possible to fight back and win."

Enola's heart swelled with pride. They were tired, battered, and bruised, but they weren't broken. Not anymore. The shadow had been defeated, and with it, the despair that had loomed over them for so long.

The rest of the gang began to murmur in agreement, their voices growing stronger. A spark of hope caught fire among them, flickering in the cool morning air. Enola turned her gaze toward the distant horizon, where the sunlight broke over the remains of the city like a promise.

But even as they began planning their next steps, Enola couldn't shake a lingering feeling. The shadow was gone, but Korr's betrayal had left its mark on her. The trust they had rebuilt would take time to heal. She resolved to confront him soon, to find out where his loyalties truly lay.

For now, though, she let herself focus on the moment. Rebuilding would be slow, but it was a beginning. They had a future to fight for, and Enola wasn't about to let it slip away.

The next few days were a blur of activity. Enola led the effort to clear debris from the streets while Rook, despite his injuries, helped organize the group into teams. They worked tirelessly, reclaiming what little they could from the ruins of their once-vibrant city.

Occasionally, they found traces of other survivors—paw prints in the dirt, faint trails of movement—but no one had yet revealed themselves. Still, the signs of life fuelled their determination. As Enola walked the quiet streets of the broken city, she paused to take in the scene around her. The rubble, the cracked pavement, the faint traces of life returning—it was all so surreal. Only a few days ago, she had crept through Little Vixen Street, scrounging for food, just another stray trying to survive. It felt like a lifetime had passed since then. In truth, the battle for the city had lasted mere days, but the weight of those moments had stretched time itself, leaving scars deeper than she could comprehend.

One evening, as the sun dipped low, Enola found herself on a crumbled rooftop overlooking the city. Her gaze swept over the gathered survivors. For a moment, she thought she caught a flash of familiar orange fur in the distance—a shape that moved like Korr, bold and determined. Her breath hitched. But when she blinked, it was gone, replaced by a swirl of morning mist dissipating in the gentle breeze.

She felt a pang in her chest, the loss fresh despite everything they had endured. Korr's absence was palpable, his boldness and strength woven into the very fabric of their journey. Though gone, his memory lingered in every decision they made and every step they took toward rebuilding.

Chapter 30

The city had never looked so quiet.

Somewhere in Enola stood at the edge of the hill overlooking Little Vixon Street, where her journey had begun. Only days ago, she had been scavenging for scraps, just another stray cat trying to survive. Now, the street was empty, its buildings casting long shadows in the morning light. The silence wasn't oppressive this time; it was peaceful, alive with the promise of something new.

Behind her, Rook limped into view, his shoulder bandaged from the wounds he'd suffered in the battle. He didn't say much, but his presence was steady, reassuring. They had all changed—scarred, wiser, but alive.

"What are you thinking about?" he asked, his voice soft.

"Back when it was just me," Enola said, her gaze distant. "Digging through trash piles, dodging humans, wondering if I'd survive another day. It feels like a lifetime ago, but it wasn't. Just a few days."

Rook sat beside her, his tail flicking lazily against the dirt. "You've come a long way. We all have."

The gang had begun to gather below. Stray cats and dogs worked together, sorting through what little remained of their supplies and patching up their makeshift shelters. Korr's absence hung heavy over them, but his sacrifice had given them a chance to rebuild.

"Do you think we'll ever be safe?" Rook asked, breaking the silence.

Enola didn't answer immediately. She thought of the shadow, its suffocating darkness, and the crystal's terrible power. They had destroyed it, but who was to say there weren't other threats lurking out there?

"I don't know," she admitted. "But I think we've proven we can face whatever comes next."

Rook nodded, his gaze distant. "Korr would've liked that."

They sat in silence for a moment longer before a distant sound caught Enola's ears—a faint rumble, almost like thunder. She straightened, her fur bristling.

"Did you hear that?" she asked.

Rook frowned. "Probably just the wind."

But it didn't feel like the wind. Enola's instincts prickled, the same way they had back in the tunnels when she'd first encountered the shadow.

Down below, one of the younger cats, a small tabby named Finch, called out. "Enola! You might want to see this!"

Enola exchanged a wary glance with Rook before hurrying down the hill. The gang was gathered around a collapsed wall, their eyes wide with alarm.

"What is it?" Enola asked, pushing her way to the front.

Finch pointed a trembling paw at the ground. At first, Enola didn't see anything unusual—just rubble and dirt. But then she noticed it: a faint glow, pulsing softly beneath the surface. It was the same eerie light she'd seen in the crystal.

"No," Rook muttered, his voice tight. "We destroyed it."

"Not all of it," Enola said grimly.

The glow brightened, and the ground beneath them trembled. Finch yelped and scrambled back as cracks began to spread outward, faint tendrils of darkness seeping through the earth.

Enola's heart pounded. The shadow was gone, but its remnants had lingered, waiting for the right moment to stir. She turned to the gang, her voice steady despite the fear tightening in her chest.

"Get everyone back to camp," she ordered. "Now."

"What about you?" Rook asked.

Enola's gaze hardened. "I'll handle this."

Rook hesitated but nodded, ushering the others away. As the gang retreated, Enola stood alone, staring at the glowing cracks.

The battle was over, but the fight wasn't. The shadow's influence ran deeper than she'd realized, its roots tangled in the heart of the city. She had thought she'd reached the end of her journey, but this was only the beginning of something larger.

As the first tendrils of darkness curled around her paws, Enola narrowed her eyes.

"Not this time," she said softly, her claws unsheathing.

The sun rose higher, its light cutting through the ruins, casting long, uncertain shadows. the distance, the faint rumble grew louder.

And Enola, once just a stray cat on Little Vixon Street, braced herself for what was to come.

About the Author

Evelyn is a passionate and avid reader and writing. Her love for books sparked the idea for her debut novel, which tells the story of cat who discovers a mysterious power and embarks on a incredible adventure. Along the way, the cat formed unexpected alliances, only to discover a shocking truth about the identity of the true enemy.

When she is not reading or writing, Evelyn enjoys exploring new worlds through fiction and imagining all the exciting possibilities stories can offer.